WICKED IN

REBEL *ink*

NEW YORK TIMES BESTSELLING AUTHOR

LAURA WRIGHT

Cover Designer: Sweet 'n Spicy Designs
by Jaycee DeLorenzo

Editor: Julia Ganis, JuliaEdits.com

Interior Designer: Jovana Shirley,
Unforeseen Editing, www.unforeseenediting.com

ISBN-13: 978-0-9861631-2-8

Contents

SELF-PROFESSED HOT BRUNETTE FROM THE BAR

He's such a prick.

A total dick.

A bastard.

And yet…I giggle softly to myself as he flips me onto my stomach, wraps his tatted hand around my wrists and thrusts inside me. He's really big, and I gasp and press my face into the folds of the black sheets of his bed. That's right, dolls. Black sheets. White pillows. Red room. Graffiti on the walls. Las Vegas penthouse.

And another girl in the mix.

In fact, her stiletto heels are bracketing my shoulders right now.

"Ass up," Vincent commands.

"But I want to see what you're doing to her," I pout on a muffled moan.

Instead of answering me though, he slams into me four times, so hard I lose my breath. Not that I'm complaining. I turn my head to pull in air, and come face to face with one of those silver stilettos. The heel is digging into the mattress as she moans above me. I can't get enough, and clearly neither can she. What was her name again? Megan? Maggie? Miz Come-Fuck-Me-Heels?

I grin through my sharp intake of breath.

Though I can't see her anymore—mean badass boy and his demands—I know she's standing over me, her pussy pressed to his face. It was so fucking hot to watch I nearly came. That's why he flipped me. He doesn't want me to come. Told me I can't.

And I always listen to Vincent.

The tall, inked and pierced, skinny-ripped sex god with black eyes that eat you up nearly as good as his tongue can—who's so completely addictive, and who has the most perfect cock I've ever seen.

That's right. Just seen.

Not touched—or sucked.

I'll never understand it. What guy in his right mind wouldn't want a girl to blow him? Or at the very least, pump him off with her very skilled hand? But that's why we all like Vincent so much, isn't it?

He's not in his right mind.

Maybe it's a superpower. The *no touch, no suck* rule. Maybe that's the secret to how he can go all night without exploding.

I grin broadly to myself, then gasp as he slides out of me.

"Noooo," I complain. Too empty.

So if I turn and wrap my hand around his cock and guide it back in where it belongs, he'll kick me out of this bed, right? My pussy clenches at the thought. Nope. Not gonna chance it. *Oh. Fuck. Yes. There you are.* He slides in again, deep—really deep—and stays there, grinding circles around my sex.

I pray he doesn't leave me again. At least not until I get off. Vincent gives the best orgasms. It's like an event with him, a blue ribbon to win every time.

And he does. Wins.

Owns.

I was with him a couple of months ago. He'd given me head after a pretty tortuous ink session on my right hipbone. Spread me out and locked me in on his fucked-up chair at Wicked Ink. I don't think he remembers though, because tonight, at the bar, when he told me and what's-her-name to come upstairs with him, he looked at me as if I was new material.

One long, lubed finger slides into my ass then, and well, that's it folks. Ass fucking is my downfall. Maybe he does remember me after all. As he starts to move again, I hear him behind me, hear his mouth working that chick over. Wet, sucking, hungry sounds that make my nipples tingle and pussy cream. Soon I'll be in the manic state. Unhinged.

"I can't hold this much longer, baby," I moan.

"Me either," the chick above me cries out. Mia? Maren?

"Put us both out of our misery, hot stuff," I beg. "Please."

"And then we'll work *you* over real good."

Good luck with that honey, I muse, my breathing so shallow I pray I don't pass out. At least before I come.

Vincent doesn't say a thing. He never does, unless it's a demand. What he wants, doesn't want. But right now, I could care less. I'm so close. My entire body is one ready and willing nerve ending. I arch my back to give him better access. He still has my wrist in one of his hands, while the fingers on the other pump my ass gently.

He's fucking me and eating her.

Behold the talent!

I hear the chick come first—Oh god! Oh God! Oh GOD!—all of which sets me off. In my mind, I see her pounding her sex against his wet mouth, and wave after wave of mind-crashing heat and pleasure erupt inside me. I can do nothing but take what he's giving me now because it's so brutal. Deliciously brutal. Like something wild. His hand tightens around my wrist and his cock swells. I think he's coming. Yet still he continues to pound.

Raw talent.

For thirty more fantastic seconds, he continues to thrust inside of me. No mercy. All pleasure.

And then its over.

Like a hot, thick blanket being ripped off my skin, he's pulling out of me. I'm wrecked, chilled, exhausted. I crumple into the sheets. Don't even attempt to turn around when I hear the chick say, "Where are you going, gorgeous? Your dick is still hard and my pussy is still wet."

Still hard?

Shit.

I'll tell her where he's going in a minute or two. When I catch my breath. I'll tell her what I know—and all that I don't about the super antihero that is Vincent. The delicious robo-cock, who gives and gives and comes—but never takes.

Poor girl won't have that cock in her tonight.

Mmmm…maybe I'll help her out. I sigh and turn over.

Muffy, Mabel, Monica…

I'm having the same dream I have pretty much every night. I'm dressed in white. Blinding white. The kind you wear when you enter heaven. The kind that hurts people's eyes if they stare directly at you. And I can tell it's hurting them because, the people standing in front of me? They're putting sunglasses on. One by one. Like, all down the row. Except my mother, of course. No sunglasses for her. She refuses. Probably because they're not Chanel. Or maybe it's because of the tears she's shedding. They're streaming down her face, causing streaks in her makeup. But they're not tears of emotion. I know this. Like, in my guts. They're from relief. I'm done. Cooked. Not her problem anymore. Or the thing that causes her worry—makes her take those little oval white pills at ten and five every day.

She can wash her hands of me. She can retreat to her white mansion by the sea and—

White.

Blinding white.

It blinds us all.

Wait…am I blind too?

"Take off your sunglasses, Lis." It's Addy now. No tears. Just the voice of reason. She's standing in front of me, a halo on her head. Her eyes, the blue one and the green one, are very clear. So clear. She's clear.

She's always clear now.

"I'm sleeping," I tell her.

"Fucking right, you are," she returns with her typical brand of sarcasm. "For like ten months now."

Ten months? That sounds like a fairy tale. A princess asleep for ten months. Of course, that would explain things. The white light…the white dress…

"You need to wake up." Addy's voice sounds so sharp. And it's close to my ear. Or her breath is. Strange. The intense light is receding. Am I still wearing a dress? I look down. Yes. But it's flecked with red snow. Oh. My mother's gone. She's run away. Far away. I'm glad for that—

Hands grip my shoulders. Cold hands.

They're shaking me.

"Dammit, Lis!" Addison hisses. "Wake the hell up. Now."

Darkness slams into the light and I jerk awake and sit up. I'm breathing heavy. Feel hot. I blink a couple of times. My room is my room, except it's bathed in soft pink light. The lamp. I turn and—Jesus, Addison is standing next to the lamp near my bed like the flippin' Grim Reaper. My heart drops into my stomach. "Oh my god." I clutch my chest like I'm seventy and at risk for a heart attack. "What are you doing here?"

"Later," she whispers. "Right now we have to go. Get up."

I stare at her and don't move. "What are you talking about? Is this the apocalypse? Are there Walking Dead heading for Montecito right now?

Because that's the only way you're getting me out of this bed."

She doesn't laugh. Doesn't even crack a smile, which is weird because we watch that show together while we Skype. Am I still dreaming? I pinch myself on the wrist to check. Dang! No. Not dreaming.

Something slams into my face. It's soft, but heavy.

"Put on your robe," she commands, "And come with me."

I pull the thing down and glance at the clock, the one I got for my twelfth birthday. It's shaped like a chicken and bawks when the alarm goes off. "It's four freaking o'clock in the morning."

"I know, grandma." She rolls her eyes and comes over to the bed, rips off the covers. "You should be ashamed, Lis. Four o'clock in the morning used to be your favorite time of day."

I frown. "I'm not in the mood for a shame spiral, Addy. Now, what the hell? Why are you in my room? Why are you in Santa Barbara at all?"

She chews her lip for a second like she's thinking. "I wanted to see you. I miss you."

"Awww, well, that's sweet and weird." I pat the mattress. "So get in here, then. Kick off the shoes. Whatever you want to talk about can wait until the morning. Then you can just stay and help me with last minute—"

"No. No sleep." The Addy of Las Vegas, the one who is all kickass now with a job at a marketing firm and a hot, crazy, tatted boyfriend, comes at me, shaking her head. She grabs my hand and tugs. "Up."

This girl is still so new to me. I wish I was more like her. I think I used to be.

"Okay," I say, jerking my hand away from her. "Clearly, you've lost your shit." I look up at her—like, really look at her. Tight jeans, black cami with a stylish red flannel over it and wedge boots. She's totally put together. Even her hair is fab—relaxed fishtail braid over one shoulder. She looks gorge. I scratch the crown of my messy white-blond bun. "What's this all about, Addy? You're really freaking me out. Breaking into the house—"

"I still remember the alarm code," she says. "And the side door off the kitchen was actually open."

"Great. I'll be keeping that tidbit to myself. Mom will totally fire Gloria if she hears." I sigh.

"You aren't supposed to be here for three more days."

Her eyes flash with something then…something of the hiding variety, and she reaches out and grabs my hand again. "I just need you."

My gut does this fish-flop thing. I don't like the look on her face. "Oh, shit. Did something happen? Is it Rush? Did he do something?"

I've been waiting for this. Rush seems like a good guy, but then again look who he hangs out with.

A flash of the dark, foul-mouthed tatted and pierced one slams into my brain. *Get out. See the Do Not Disturb sign? That's for you.*

"It's not Rush," Addy says. "It's me. I have to talk to you, Lis. Please come out to the car with me. Just for a quick drive."

She can always make me cave. I love her ass too damn much. I stand up and stretch. "If you want to talk, we can go to the pool house or something," I slip my robe on over my sweats and tank top, then re-work the bun on top of my head.

"I need to drive. I know that's crazy since I've been driving for hours. But…there it is."

"Oh…*fine*." I sigh, tired and slightly annoyed, but I step into my UGG boots and head for the door. I mean, she is my bestie of all time.

She follows me out of my room and down the long stretch of hallway, which is gently lit from inside the glass that's built into the crown molding. We're quiet as we descend the marble staircase. But honestly no one can really hear us in this part of the house. Our housekeeper and maid both sleep two floors above me in the west wing. And my parents have the entire east wing to themselves. But I still don't want to risk it. They're not too keen on Addy these days. Actually, they were never all that keen on her. Wrong side of the tracks—and by that I mean anywhere outside of Montecito and *maybe*, if they're feeling generous, the Santa Barbara Riviera.

Addy is parked in the very center of our circular driveway. Girl has grown some serious balls in the past year. And her ride confirms it. She drives a screaming hot Porsche now. A prezzie from her rich boyfriend. Which is good. She deserves it. She's never known what money feels like. How good and safe and comfortable it feels.

Or how hard it is to give up.

The minute I close the car door and click my seatbelt into place, she takes off. Montecito is completely dead at this time of night. Dark and chilly, stars blinking in and out of the cover of trees. We hit the 101, which is Addy's fave because it trails the ocean. Even at night, you can see the heavy black waves crashing against the rocks. The air is salty and cold, and I breathe it in to wake myself up.

"So, what's going on?" I ask. "What's got you driving to the SB from Vegas in the middle of the night? Can't be good."

"It's not," she agrees.

Okayyy… I give her a minute or two to drop whatever bomb she's holding, but when we pass the Summerland exit, my gut tenses. I roll up my window and face her. "We better be getting off in Carp and coming right back again."

She doesn't say a word.

My pulse speeds up a little. "Okay, whore!" I say. "Spill it or I'm going to…jump out of this car."

"No you won't."

Course I won't, but I'm nothing without my empty threats. Seriously.

She chews her top lip a second, then just as we pass the first Carpentaria exit, she turns to me. "You're coming back to Vegas with me."

I stare. Then I laugh. "Umm, no I'm not. I'm getting married in five days."

"Yeah, about that…" she begins.

"Addy," I start, my laughter dying a quick death.

She doesn't answer.

"Addy!"

Just reaches over and hits the child safety locks.

VINCENT

"What happened last night?" Rush asks me, about one fucking second after I walk in the door at Wicked Ink. He's standing behind reception with Janie, whose eyeballs continue to track the computer screen.

Smart girl.

Or she couldn't give a shit about my night.

Again. Smart girl.

"I got a customer coming in at ten," I say, heading straight for my room. Don't have time for this. Never do.

Not that it stops him. He's been going all owner/manager on my ass lately. It's bullshit.

Five seconds inside my dungeon, and he's there in the doorway. "You're late. Again."

"It's 9:50, Merrick," I say, although I hate having to answer to him. About anything. Even more so lately.

"We had a staff meeting at nine. You said you'd be there."

"Did I?"

"Yeah, dickhead. You did."

"You wanna fire me?"

Rush exhales all rough and pissed off. "Shit, man. This is getting old."

"Hey! That's what Addison says." My mouth twitches.

Impervious to my real pointed insult that involves his girl, he comes all the way in now. Like I invited his ass. Which I didn't.

"I don't want to fire you, V," he says, dropping himself down on the arm of my red couch. "I want to know what's happening."

I pause over my tray, take inventory. "Nada."

"Bullshit," he presses.

"Seriously. All's cool, brother."

"I just don't buy it. I know you, V."

I shake my head. Boy is so clueless. He knows what I want him to know. Nothing more. Nothing less. And nothing in between.

"Did you knock someone up?" he asks.

I snort and start wiping down my electric chair and restraints. Not that clients use the latter, but I like to give 'em the option.

"Doing some meth?" Rush continues to pester. "Blow?"

"Fuck me," I grind out.

"Special K? Bath salts?"

That last bit is his attempt at a joke, so I glance up from my tools of torture and toss him the brow. "You know my drug of choice, Merrick. P is for Pussy, baby. Can't help myself, you know? It's like a new crop just came in and I have to sample. Every night something different. Something better." I sorta bow my head. "Sorry, man."

He stares at me, hard, for a just a second or two, then blows out a breath. "Fine. Whatever, manwhore. Just stop with the late shit, okay—"

"No," I interrupt. "Not sorry for the clock. Sorry for being such an epic fucking stud while you're…you know, ball-and-chaining it."

He flips me off. "I know you're not giving me the true scoop. You've been screwing your way through Vegas for five years, V. And most of

Southern Nevada. Never made you perpetually late before." His brows go up. His turn to mock my ass. And it's some pretty good shit. "You getting old?"

I grin, then turn back to my tray.

"Maybe you need to schedule your three-ways at six p.m." Rush continues. "Like, right after the early bird special."

"Maybe."

"I know this ain't all about getting laid."

"I'm having fun. Remember that? Fun?" I glance over my shoulder. "Don't hate on us single dudes, Merrick. Not my fault you're stuck fucking the same skirt every night."

His jaw gets tight, and my grin widens.

"You're such an ass," he says.

Oh, tell me something I don't know. "And you're running on a clock now that you're married and shit."

"I'm not married. Yet."

"Whatever. This ain't no brokerage firm, Merrick. No nine-to-five, working lunches bullshit." I run a hand through my silver-tipped fauxhawk. Maybe it's time for a shave. "I may miss one of your precious meetings from time to time because, fuck, who wouldn't? But I never leave a client waiting."

I can feel him staring at me. Like, shooting fire daggers into my back. Into one of the pieces he inked. I think he's taking it all in, wanting to believe what I say—all the three-way boasting—cuz he knows what a whore I am…but he's not entirely there. And I need him to believe me. Actually, what

I need is him to fuck the hell off and let me deal with my…shit…in my own way.

Fucking women. Lots of women.

Satisfies the body and numbs the mind.

Well, it used to.

Lately…

I finish mixing my black and gray—start cleaning my tat gun. "I got La Salle coming in five minutes. Lots of shit to prepare. So either fire my ass or get the fuck out and let me do my job."

I give him five seconds to speak before I flip on HAVOK and turn the speakers up to deaf.

Lisa

"How long are you going to not talk to me?" Addy asks as around us the sky is a perfect blue and the landscape is nothing but desert. "I mean, no pressure or anything. I'm just curious. Like…rough estimate?"

Once again, I palm my iPhone and type. Then I lift it up and turn it for her to read: *Bring me back to Santa Barbara, whore! Now!*

"Sorry," she says. "No can do. Besides, we're thirty minutes from home."

I huff. She's bonkers. Again I type: *Not my home!*

"For the next few days it will be." She glances over at me, tosses me one of her serious looks.

She's been doing that a lot lately. "You need this, Lis."

What you're doing is illegal!

She snorts. "How do you figure?"

BRIDENAPPING, BITCH! Then I emphasize this with an open-mouthed '*Seriously!*' stare.

"So, like, you'll have me arrested if we stop?" She turns back to the road, grinning. "Or if a cop pulls us over?"

With a groan of irritation, I give up. The typing is becoming totes tedious, and well, I'm just a talker by nature. I'm too into inflections and air quotes to be suppressed in this way. I turn my body toward her and try to reason. "I have a hundred things to do, Addy. The wedding is five days away. What exactly are you playing at?"

"Your wedding to Buttons." It's all she says. Still staring at the road.

RUDE.

"Okay, don't call him that," I say.

"*You* called him that. As well as 'The Tongue,' 'Life Stealer,' and 'Wouldn't Know What To Do With A Vagina If It Was Staring Him In The Face.'"

My jaw gets all tight and I turn to face the road too. "That was months and months ago. Before I really got to know him."

"So he knows what to do with a vagina now?"

"You're gross."

"And you can't be serious about this. About him!"

"He's a good man, Addy. Zero drama. You just refuse to see that because he's simple and uncomplicated and doesn't have tattoos and wear all black."

She snorts. "Oh, yeah, that's why I don't see it."

"This is not cool, bestie." I turn and look at her. She's hurting my feelings now. Not just because she's insulting the man I'm about to marry, but because she should have my back—no matter what. "This is why I've eased up on the texting and the visiting, just FYI. I'm tired of your negativity."

She doesn't back down. I'm a little surprised, but I guess this is the new and kickass Addison now. "Not because you don't want to face the fact that you invited me without a plus one?"

"Oh my god," I say with real frustration. How many times can we go over this? Seriously? "That was not my decision and you know it. My parents took care of the invite list." Along with everything else.

Suddenly, she jerks the wheel to the right. I gasp and grip the door handle. She pulls up along the side of the freaking freeway and stops. Just stops. Idles.

I turn to stare at her. "Well this isn't dangerous or anything."

"Do you actually hear yourself, Lis?" she says, eyes narrowed. "Not your decision?"

"What I mean is that they're paying—"

"On who you get to invite to YOUR wedding? And since when has anything not been your decision? I mean, what the hell? Rush is my fiancé. And I'm your best friend. Or I used to be."

"This has nothing to do with you and me. My parents—"

"Oh my god! What have you become?"

I turn and face the front, cross my arms over my chest. "A prisoner, apparently." I don't want to hear anymore. It's starting to really get to me.

"Well, I'm not the one who made you that way. It's like an alien has taken over your body. First with Buttons—"

"Stop calling him that. He's going to be my husband!"

She slaps the steering wheel. "You thought he was a total goof. White bread served up by your parents. Now you're marrying him, settling in Montecito a few mansions down from your parents. Hey—and your parents. They're calling all the shots."

"Again, they're paying, Addy. They get to call all the shots."

"This is your wedding!" she shouts. "Your day! Your choice! Your life!"

"No, it's not!" I shout back. Then I freeze because I hear what I just said, and it makes me feel a little sick. It's not like I don't know what I'm allowing. It's not like I don't remember the girl I used to be in college not even a year ago—the drive and ambition and belief I had in myself. But I've seen what I'm capable of and what I'm not. I don't have the thing—the gene, the whatever it is that makes a person able to stand on their own and persevere through adversity. I tried and I failed. No job except the ones that pay minimum wage, and that nearly made me homeless.

So I quit and went running home to Mom and Dad.

And Kevin Stanfield.

Aka Buttons.

He's really a decent guy. Okay, he's weak. Sure. But then again, so am I.

"Listen," I say. "If you abducted me in an attempt to reprogram my alien mind and/or get me to call off the wedding, you might as well just drop my hot ass at the nearest gas station and I'll get home on my own. This wedding is happening. It's what I want. I wish you could have my back, accept this, and just play along. But I'll understand if you can't."

For several long seconds, I watch Addy stare out the window as cars and semis whiz past and make the car shiver. Am I going to the gas station? Is she not going to be my maid of honor?

Then she releases a weary breath. "Okay. Fine."

"Fine?" I repeat, surprised.

She turns and nods. "But I don't want you to go. Can you stay a couple days?" She gives me a crooked smile. "We can change the abduction to a bachelorette party."

The heaviness in my heart lessens. Or lightens, maybe. Whatever it is, I'm just grateful. For Addy's acquiescence, and for a little time to spend with her. It's been a lot of months since I've been here. I sit up and flip down the mirror on my visor. "Jesus Christ, this won't do. All I have is my purse. If we're going to do this, I'll need different clothes."

"For sure." Addison shifts out of neutral. "You're a hot mess in that get-up."

I smile at her. My best friend. "Well at least I'm hot."

The mess part…well, no one needs to know about that right now.

She smiles back, then checks her mirror and hauls ass back onto the freeway.

VINCENT

I'm busted. Two hours of shitty sleep after a fuck session that was supposed to get me five, then a half day spent bent over a dude's flesh, making sure each line is up to my standards. I need to pass the hell out. But once again my phone's blowing up. She won't leave me alone. I've changed my number three times, but she keeps calling.

I push out of my chair and stand, stretch my back. Station looks so clean you could operate in here. Sometimes it feels like I do. I grab my phone off the tray and delete the message without even listening to it because I know what it says. Same thing it's said for the past six weeks.

Come.

Now.

I need you.

I miss you.

Texts, emails, calls to the crib. She won't call here, to Wicked Ink. It's my one blessing.

I head for the couch and fall back onto the leather, toss my arm over my eyes. Maybe it'll happen here. *Sleep, bitch.* Maybe I can find a way to turn off the movie screen in my head. The horror flick. Fucking hasn't done it. Not really. Maybe when I come. Maybe for those few seconds I'm out…

Pussy. *What the fuck's wrong with you that you can't just pass the hell out?*

I rip my arm away and stare at the ceiling.

I hear Janie's voice in the reception area. It's all high and girly, which isn't her thing at all. She's a pretty tough chick. Like, the kind who can hang with guys like me and not faint or run or want to bone me. Not that I didn't think about it when she first came here. But then, you know, we made friends.

Her laughter snakes under my door. What the fuck? Maybe it's a dude she's hot for. One of those rockers who wait for-freaking-ever on her list just to get under her.

Her needle, that is.

With a grunt and a *fuck me*, I sit up and get my ass off the couch. No nap for poor little Vincent. Clearly he needs another full night of shagging. With three skirts instead of two. Go long or go home.

And then don't sleep. Again.

I bust out my door. I'm curious who Janie's talking up, but I also need coffee. Like a full pot, grounds included. I have one more 'operation' today. A cover-up—and I don't fuck around with that shit.

"Hey, Vincent."

Oh. It's only Addison. The ball and the chain.

But then I hold on a second…cuz no, it's not just the BC, it's also the B—Blondie. And the Pain in my A. And the very hot T's. And the one chick in this world who has actually said no to me.

Much respect, yo.

"You remember Lisa," Addison says.

"Sure, I remember." I stop near the group of three chicks and look the blond one up and down. She's wearing sweats, a robe, and—good goddamn I hate these things—Ugg-ly boots. It's like wearing two dirty sheep on your feet. "What the hell happened to you?"

I expect her to go all shocked and disgusted at my obvious insult. But she smiles kinda like she feels sorry for me. "Ah, yes, Vincent. Such a gentleman."

"He's just tired," Addy explains. "Rush said he's out gutter trolling all night long."

Janie regards me with curiosity. "But he's always done that." She cocks her head. "What's wrong, pumpkin? What can sissy Janie do to help?"

"Fuck you, Red," I grind out, and she laughs. Then I turn back to Addison and give her the death stare—which never works. "Rush shouldn't be talking to you about me at all, BC."

"BC?" Lisa looks at Addison.

"Ball and Chain," Addison provides. "It's his pet name for me."

"Awww, that's so sweet," Lisa says.

Addison smiles. "I know, right?"

I wonder why I'm still standing here. *Like, seriously, numbnuts, go get your flippin' coffee already.* And yet, I don't move. Can't help myself. I'm curious why Blondie's back here after all this time. Been nearly a year since that Cali graduation Rush dragged my ass to. And why's she dressed for bed—well, the bed of a chick who's pretty much given up and married her cat. For fuck's sake, it's like three o'clock in the afternoon.

"Are you guys going shopping?" Janie asks them.

"Definitely," Lisa says. "I can't be seen like this for much longer."

"You ain't kiddin'," I say. At least she recognizes there's a problem. That is step one.

"Vincent, dearest," Janie coos, casting me a stop-fucking-with-this-chick smile. "Perhaps you have things to do?"

"No. I'm good."

Lisa rolls her eyes. Oh, yeah. I remember the eye roll. She does that same thing when you ask her to join you and another chick in the sack. It's real turn-on. *Not.*

"So, what's the plan?" Janie asks them.

"I don't know for sure," Addison tells her. "Strip club? Dance club?"

"Sex club?" I offer.

Janie looks like she wants to clock me. "Zip the lip, V."

Speaking of lips, Lisa's top one is curled to the max. As in pissed off. The thing'd look good pierced. I remember thinking that the first time we met. Both the top and bottom are real nice and full. Would take a metal ring easy, and sexy.

"This all sounds kind of shady," I remark. I'm just so damn comfortable where I am. "What are you two doing anyway? And does PW know about this?"

Lisa sighs. "I don't want to ask. Really, I don't. I should just ignore it. And yet…"

"PW is Pussy Whipped," Addison supplies.

"Ah. Of course."

"But he is, though," Vincent says. "Right, Blondie? I mean, you see it too?"

She ignores me. “How about dancing? Since Janie’s busy tonight, the party will just be the two of us, but that’s okay. It’ll be like old times.”

Addison smiles so damn sweetly at her sad sack of a friend it hurts my teeth. “I wish we could get your other friends from the SB here.”

“It’s fine.” Lisa digs in her purse and takes out her cell. “They’re barely friends, anyway. They’re actually Kevin’s friends, to be honest.”

“Who’s Kevin?” I catch myself asking. Why I should give a shit about any of this malarkey is beyond me, but it’s already out my gob, so…

She’s typing something on her iPhone. When she’s done, she looks up at me. “If you must know, he’s my fiancé.”

Yeah. Sounds about right. You know, she's like twenty-one. Genius time to legally bind yourself to someone. "So, you're getting married?"

"That's usually what you do with a fiancé," she returns with some attitude.

Hmm. I like this Lisa. I could even get past the sweatpants if this Lisa was on the menu. Course, the Ugg-lies would have to go. Like, permanently.

"In five days," Addison tells me.

Five… Well, shit. That's done. Off the menu.

Rush and his client are just leaving his room. Brother's got a pretty significant Band-Aid on his shoulder. Wonder what the boss laid down on him. Looks like a dragon or a tiger kind of bloke. They say a quick goodbye and then Rush hightails it over to Addison and snakes an arm around her waist.

"Hey, baby. I missed you in my bed this morning." While I upchuck in my mouth a little, his lips go to her ear and he kisses her. Then he spots Lisa and grins. "So. The abduction took place." He squeezes Addison and she gasps. "My sexy little lawbreaker."

She glances over her shoulder at him and gives him a smile I've never seen. Clearly it's reserved only for the boss man. And that's A-OK.

"I still have the cuffs," she says. "She didn't require them."

He grins. "Well fuck, I do. Tonight."

"No can do, sir." She pretends to look sad. Or is that a pout?

Shit, I shouldn't be looking. Or caring.

"Tonight is Lisa's bachelorette party. We're about to go shopping for our super-slutty outfits right now."

Oh! There it is. I knew I was sticking around for something. "Tell me about these outfits?" I say, leaning against the recep desk, like I ain't going nowhere.

Addison laughs. "Nothing as hardcore as the gutter rats you're used to, Vincent."

I turn to glare at Merrick. "What the fuck you been telling your girl, man?"

"Just the truth as I see it," he responds, though his eyes and attention are totally focused on Addison.

"We should go," she says to him, then lifts her chin. "Kiss me."

As Rush obliges, pulling her into his arms and getting right to the sucking face, Lisa glances my way. She nods.

"Vincent."

"Blondie."

She presses her lips together. "So not nice seeing you again." Then she turns and heads for the front door.

I shake my head as I watch her go. She's still such a smartass. And she still doesn't like me. Oh, damn…why do I find that so fucking hot? Smartass and hatred: clearly two of my favorite qualities in a chick. Plus the being hot and having big tits. And a tight ass, of course.

As I push away from the recep desk that Janie is now behind, running over her schedule on the computer, Rush and Addison practically fuck each other right there on the floor. Hands groping, mouths working. Thank Christ she pulls away before the clothes start coming off. I enjoy a good show from time to time, but watching my friend and his BC get it on in the middle of Wicked…nope. Pass.

"You got it bad, man," I tell him as Addison follows Lisa out of the shop.

Rush adjusts his denim. "No. What I got is a hard fucking cock."

This makes me laugh. "So. Come out with me tonight," I suggest. "I'll make sure you get that taken care of."

"Shit," Rush breathes, shaking his head.

"You are a sick bastard with no morals, V," Janie calls out from behind the reception desk.

Rush points at her. "What she said."

“So that a yes?” I ask.

His eyes roll. But he’s interested. I can see it. Maybe not for the dipping his pen in another inkpot idea, but hanging out. It’s been a long time. Before the BC we used to have a fucking great time. I miss those days. It can get lonely…even in a threesome.

“I’ll go out with you,” Rush says after a minute. “But it ain’t like that,” he continues. “I got a girl, my one and only, love of my fucking life—”

“Yeah, yeah. I get it. Let’s not encourage the puke to rise up any higher in my throat, okay?”

Janie glances up from the computer. “You’re vile.”

I ignore her. “So…what are we doing then, Andy Griffith?”

“You ever crash a bachelorette party before?”

"Yup." I know right where he's going, and I'm already shaking my head. "But I don't want to crash this one."

"Come on," Rush implores me.

"No way."

"I gotta see my baby in her slutty outfit, man."

I laugh. Sometimes the dude is funny.

"And you like Lisa," he continues. "Or did."

"No," I correct. "I wanted to fuck Lisa. While we both pussy-snacked a couple of other chicks."

"Jesus Christ on a cracker, Vincent!" Janie says.

It's Rush's turn to shake his head at me.

"What?" I ask.

"You've gotten worse," he says. "Right, J?"

"Like, beyond, Boss. Heavy duty, counseling-in-Utah or somewhere kinda thing."

I grin at them both. Their oh-so-lovable insults have pretty much retooled my mood. Shoved some shit back—shit I've been trying to pretend doesn't exist. And I'm real grateful.

"Listen," Rush says, checking his phone. "I'm done for the day. I'm going home to clean myself up, make my ass presentable. You in, meet me there at nine. You out, don't be late tomorrow."

Without another word, he heads back into his room to pack his shit up.

"I second that," Janie pipes up from behind the desk.

I turn around and loom over the desk. "What are you going on about?"

"The don't-be-late thing. We're doing a piece together tomorrow, remember?"

"Course I remember." My eyebrows go up and down. "Five eleven, never wears a bra—"

"She's married, V. To the lead singer of Interbreed."

I shrug. "Point?"

She glares up at me, her red lips all pouty as she contemplates explaining things to me. Finally she just gives up, exhales loudly and returns to the computer. "Just be here, my beloved manwhore friend, okay?"

I push away from the desk. "Well, when you sweet-talk me like that…"

Shaking her head, she laughs, and I make a break into the back for coffee. On the way my ass starts buzzing. I yank it out.

My place. 9:00p.m. Be there or you're fired – Your dickhead boss

I chuckle and flip him off, then stick the thing back in my pocket and grab my ACDC mug. Coffee's hot and thick. I'm gonna get wired, yo. Need to. Both to perfectly paint my client, and drive that Lisa chick out of my head.

Again.

I down half the brown goodness and burn my tongue.

Fuck.

Blondie.

Leave it to her to make me injure one of my most prized assets. Whoever is having the misfortune of shacking up with that train wreck in a track suit—okay, sweats, but give it five years—has my condolences. Forget the sarcasm and California princess routine—she's probably one of those back-to-the-mattress, legs-spread, bra-on, zero alerts that she's coming, making-the-guy-work nightmares.

You dodged a bullet, my friend.

Mug in hand, I head out of the break room. Once again, my ass buzzes. I shake my head and grab the phone from my pocket. Pushy asshole. Probably wants to wear matching outfits or some shit. And just to be a team player, I might oblige him.

But the text's not from him.

> *I am devastated that you refuse to speak to me. Shall I beg? Is that what you want? Please, Vincent. I need you here. Tomorrow night at—*

I don't read any more. Delete. Delete. Delete.

Jaw tight, I stalk into my dungeon and slam the door. Forget the coffee now—I'm wired in a whole other way now. In a way that ain't good for my art.

I need to chill.

Let this pass—forget about it.

I have a customer coming in five, and he's going to get my best work, whatever the fuck it takes.

I turn my phone off and toss it on the couch.

No more calls, texts or emails tonight.

From anyone.

Dressed like two Vegas call girls—the high-class ones, of course—Addy and I are sitting side by side in the back of a black stretch limo she rented. *Love her*! We're moving down the Strip easy peasy because traffic is a bitch and a half. But that's okay by me. Because, first of all, it's fun to people- and places-watch at night. And second, I need a few more seconds to finish this text.

"Please put that away," Addy begs.

Again.

I know. It's a total asshole move. And I've been at it for five minutes straight. But I kinda don't have a choice.

I glance up from the screen of my iPhone and give her a sheepish look. "They want to know where I am."

"So tell them," she says.

Sure, that's one option, I suppose.

Addison knows me too damn well. "What? You're not going to tell them you're in Las Vegas?"

Oh...*complicated*!! "The thing is," I begin. "They would sort of like it if I stayed away from here." Addy cocks her head to one side and narrows her eyes. This means she's about to go the fuck off—which I totally get—but I stop her with a quick, "It's not you. It's...sort of...well, the company you keep."

She crosses her arms over her chest. "Bad influence on you, huh?"

"It's *their* opinion," I clarify. "And I don't want to deal with the fallout, okay? I just want to have fun." She's staring at me. Like she's never really seen me before. Or maybe like I'm a bug she's inspecting. I don't like it. I look down at my phone and finish the text. Send it. "There. I've told them I'm at a spa."

"Where?"

I look up again. "Napa."

"Perfect." And with that dash of irritated-slash-disappointed sarcasm, she turns to face the lights of the Luxor Hotel.

"Addy."

She doesn't look at me.

"I know you think I've sold out, and that Kevin isn't right for me—and I'm allowing my parents to make choices for me…" I inhale and release it. It's as heavy as my heart right now. "But it's really the right thing. The best thing." *The only thing.* "I've come to understand that over these past months."

She doesn't say anything for a few seconds. Then she turns to look at me. "I don't think you've sold out, bestie. I think you've given up. And way too fast. I mean, how long were you in L.A.? Like, a hot minute?"

"Try six months."

"That's nothing. A job just doesn't fall into someone's lap right out of college—"

"I did have a job. I could barely pay my rent."

"I'm talking about the right job."

She's said this all before. I didn't want to hear it then either. "Look I couldn't do it, okay Addy? Six months of company brass telling me I didn't have what it takes—for the mailroom or an internship. Six months of dodging my landlord and eating ramen noodles. It wasn't for me. I'm too…soft."

"I don't believe that."

"You don't need to. All you need to do is be my friend." I force a smile as the limo pulls up to the club and stops. "Can you do that?"

Her eyes, one blue and one green, lined expertly in black and silver, study me. Then she reaches out and takes my hand. "Let's go get drunk and dance with hot men at the spa, shall we?"

I laugh and nod. We scramble out of the limo, thank our driver and make a beeline for the crowd gathered in front of the club.

Seizure, which is located in the Carlisle Hotel, just opened last month and Addison told me it was the perfect place to start our adventure. After we flash our I.D.'s and walk through the door I instantly feel the SB start to peel off me like cheap—or not so cheap—paint. A year ago, there was nothing I loved more than getting dressed up and going to a party. Unless it was snagging the attention of every dude in the room. Now I have company, or competition, in what had always been an unusual place. Although gorgeous, Addy had always been a chill, understated dresser. But not anymore. With her hair long and curled into a sexy/messy style, three-inch black Louboutins, and a few tattoos peeking out of her black, strapless mini dress, she's stunning. Every guy—and a few girls—are checking her out. Me, on the other hand? I'm not getting much attention. I'm wearing red and my breasts are barely covered. My heels are shockingly high and my white-blond hair is swept across my face in a deep part. I realize I'm wearing my engagement ring and take it off, put it in my purse. *Let's see what that does.*

"Should we head to the bar first?" Addy asks. "Get a little drinkie-poo?"

"Absolutely." Frankly, I haven't had any real drinks in months. My parents are big fans of either champagne or wine spritzers, and Kevin is a Merlot Man.

We sidle up to the bar. I'm incredibly gifted at sidling, and when I catch a man looking at me with appreciation, I grin. "Hello there."

He grins too. He's tall, tan and gorgeous. Clearly, the ring off is the answer.

"I love your shoes," he says in a very affected voice that instantly makes my shoulders drop. "What size?"

"Umm, eight?"

He turns to the man sitting beside him, who is not as tall, but equally as gorgeous. "Would my feet look enormous in those, Steven?"

The man laughs. "Honey, you're an eleven. Own it." He winks. "And prove it to me tonight."

I think I'm frowning, which is terrible for the facial muscles. No matter what my mother advises I don't want to start Botox until thirty.

"Lis!" Addy calls, motioning me over to a free spot she's managed to score at the bar.

I give the hot, gay boys a smile and head over to my friend. "I want to go home," I say immediately.

She laughs. "Don't be insane."

"I'm pretty sure I look…uncute."

She scrunches up her face. “What are you talking about, whore? You’re the most beautiful girl in here.”

“Well, the second,” comes a sexy, masculine voice behind us.

Recognizing it instantly, Addy whirls around and lights up like a Christmas tree. “Rush!”

Perfect. Addy’s insanely hot, tatted-up man is here. Another dude to admire her, while I attract more undesirables. Aka no one.

I turn back to face the bar. I need a margarita with salt like…fifteen minutes ago.

“What are you doing here?” Addy asks him. “You know this is females only.”

“I know, baby. And I swear I’m not about to get all in your business. But fuck, you look hot.”

She giggles. “Seriously. You need to go.”

"Can't. We're here for my bachelor party."

"Isn't that supposed to be the night before you get married?"

"Sure. You wanna get hitched tomorrow?"

She laughs. "You idiot."

"Damn, your rejection is like a knife to my heart. Not to mention certain other parts of my anatomy."

"I promise to kiss them all and make them feel better," Addy says. "Later. Now go. Wait—who's the 'we' celebrating your potential marriage to me?"

My heart plummets because I know. I soooo know. Jesus, where the hell is my drink? No. Where's the bartender so I can order? Please, can we pretend this isn't happening?

But it happens anyway. In a blaze of glory and asshole.

"Evenin', fuckers," comes the voice that once upon a time sort of rocked both my dreams and my nightmares.

Vincent strides up to the bar in tight black jeans, a nice gray long-sleeved t-shirt and combat boots. He ignores me completely, and orders a shot from one of the bartenders, who, I swear to god, hasn't even once looked my way or come over to ask me what I want.

What the hell is going on with me tonight?

And…is it just tonight?

"You just killed my buzz, Rush," I say as the owner of Wicked Ink leans against the bit of bar to my left.

He smirks. "He won't bother you. I promise."

"That's right, sweet tits." Vincent turns to regard me with a lift of the brows. "I'm here to score tail, not go after some Rolex-wearing, white bread, 'money so fat it can't fit into the Prada wallet his mommy bought him last Christmas' dude's old lady."

"That was a mouthful," I say dryly. *DRINK!!*

His black eyes flash. "That's what *she* said."

I recoil. "Gross."

"Actually, what *they* said," he corrects.

As if he needs to. *We get it—you think you're a walking, talking, bullshit-spewing stud farm.* And just like that—to prove it to me—two women come sauntering up to the bar, *clearly* on stud patrol. I would know, because I've done the exact same thing a time or two. Hungry eyes, lustful grins, booty shake with each stride. Used to be a bit of a master, really. I watch with admiration as they order drinks—WTF? Where is mine?!?—then turn to admire the gorgeous, six-foot-two, fauxhawk-wearing, tatted-up dickhead.

"You two here to party?" he asks.

They giggle. I roll my eyes.

Then I kind of wonder if that used to be me. I recognize the hair flipping move. And the lip pout. God, I used to be so on point.

"Absolutely," says the one on the right. She almost could pass for Vincent's sister. Same coloring, same black eyes and sharp-angled face. He's so perverted he probably likes that.

I turn to face Addy. "What are we doing?" Cause I know we aren't drinking.

She gives Rush a look, then reaches for my hand. "Whatever you want, Bride-to-Be."

"Let's dance," I say. "I need to get my sweat on."

She whoops. "Fuck, yeah!" She tosses Rush a goodbye wink and drags me onward. "I thought you'd never ask, beeyotch."

THE BRIDE AND THE BACHELORETTE

I can't touch. Him or her. I promised Alan. He said if I got with any more people before the wedding, he'd call it off. And that's not happening. We just bought the house in Vail.

But I can watch.

This guy, this absolutely deliciously terrifying specimen, led us into a club bathroom and locked the door. Frankly, I don't know how he did it. And why no one is banging the thing down. I imagine there are security cameras in here. But he doesn't seem to care. Neither does Michelle.

Bitch.

I'm so jealous of her right now I can barely breathe. Her skirt is up around her waist and she's straddling The Tatted One. He's holding her up against the marble wall, his mouth on her right tit while he's fucking the shit out of her. Every now and then she opens her eyes and looks at me. Grinning through her ecstasy.

Bitch.

My panties are so wet I think I'll have to go up and change them before we head to the Bellagio. We're seeing "O" later tonight. The irony is not lost on me.

Michelle's moans are getting louder. She's not looking at me anymore. The Tatted One's head is up and he's watching her. Even as she comes, he just watches her.

I wish Alan would do that to me.

I wish Alan would make me come once in awhile.

He should rub that gold card against my clit.

That might do it.

As I stare, my nipples hard against the cups of my push-up bra, Michelle comes. The Tatted One slams into her a couple more times, then pulls out. And like he's done this a million times, pulls off his condom, drops it in the trash—all without a word.

"Wait," Michelle says, breathless, her eyes glassy. "You didn't—"

He gives her a look that would make my fiancé piss his pants.

"You're still hard." Smiling coyly, she drops to her knees. "Let me take care of that."

He zips his fly as he turns around and walks out. And as the door clicks shut, I realize the only thing he said to us was, "You two here to party?"

VINCENT

I'm done.

This club is bullshit.

The chicks here are bullshit too.

She wanted to suck your dick, fool. What's bullshit about that?

I ignore myself. Myself is pretty much bullshit too. *Myself* is kinda losing it. Like, one day at a time. Like, sinking into the abyss kind of losing it.

Those fucking phone calls and texts. Why can't she leave me be? Better yet, forget I exist? It'd been promised. Once upon a fucking time. I hate people who go back on their word. Especially when the words are, "You're dead to me."

Pussies.

I drop back another shot. Where the fuck is Rush? I mean, I'm gone for what…? Twenty minutes and he skates? I swivel in my seat and run my gaze over the dance floor. Those two chicks are nutters—and not the ones I was holed up in the bathroom with. Addison and Blondie. Blondie cuz she's about to say *I do* to some Santa Barbara blue-blood douchenozzle, and she's rubbing up and down some stranger, and Addison cuz she ain't doing anything to stop it. My lips twitch. That Lisa chick is hot and all, but she's…I don't know—*off*—since the last time I saw her. At that graduation Rush forced me to go to in Santa Barbara Cali. Dude paid for that in so many ways. She seems uncomfortable in her skin, maybe. Doesn't know how to use it anymore.

Whatevs. I turn back and order another drink. This was a mistake. Coming here, trying to hang out with a friend. I'm not good at that anymore. Like Blondie, my shit ain't working right.

"Where are all your lovely dates?"

That voice is like nails down…well, in an alternate universe, my back. I grin into my third shot of whisky and turn just in time to see Lisa of Santa Barbara drop onto the barstool beside me.

"Where's the douche you were dry-humping?" I toss back.

She sighs. "Addy made him go away, and then Rush cut in and she took over in the dry-humping department. I figured I wasn't needed."

"Third ball?"

"Eleventh toe."

I sniff a little laugh at that, then gesture for another round to the nearest bartender. This one happens to be a very hot chick. Might be nice to let the snake feed again tonight—maybe even release its venom.

"Vincent?"

"Yup?"

"Do I…" she sorta stutters. "Am I…"

I turn to look at her. When she still doesn't say anything, I sigh. "Spit it out, sweet tits."

Her shoulders sag. "Do you have to use that kind of language?"

"Is that the question?"

She swivels to face me now, her whole body, crossing her long, tanned legs like a debutante. "Can you not be…*you* for just a second? I have a serious question."

I hold up one finger. If I'm going to hear something serious from Blondie, I'll need something to dull my senses…or my hearing. I toss back the shot, gesture to the barkeep for two more—one for me and one for Blondie, cuz I'm not a complete fuckface—then eye her again and raise a brow.

"Okay," she starts dramatically. "Here goes."

Jesus. So much work…

"Am I…" She shrugs. "Unattractive?"

Chicks. "To me? Or in general?"

She fails to see the humor and gets instantly uptight. "Oh forget it."

Chicks.

The bartender sets both drinks down in front of me and with my index finger I slide one over to Lisa. Lisa—she looks like such a fucking mopey dope right now. Why is the job of patching her emotional, insecure tire falling to me? *Addison, get your ass over here.*

Oh that's right. Rush has his hands on it right now.

"You're attractive, okay?" I say. Done. Over.

"Okay."

I eye her. Still facing me, drink in her hand. Shoulders slumping, frowny face. Definitely not over. "Oh, come on. Don't do that."

"Do what?"

"That girl thing where you say everything's cool but it's really not cool cuz you can't face what you're feeling—or to get the guy to probe further. Either way, I hate that shit."

She's quiet for a second. But I'm pretty sure that when she speaks again, she's going to tell me to go fuck myself. Which would be my cue to stand up and get the hell out of here. But she actually surprises me. She drains her shot, drops the empty on the bar and leans in. I can smell her perfume.

"The thing is," she begins. "I used to be sort of the center of attention at stuff like this. I kind of counted on it. Needed it." She drags her teeth across her upper lip which makes my cock twitch against my zipper.

Down, boy. That ain't no place for you.

"Granted, that's another issue all unto itself," she continues. "But anyway…I walk in here tonight and…nothing. It's like I'm one of many. Or nothing special at all. Is my dress boring? Is my makeup wrong? Is it caked on? Do I look old? Am I—"

"Jesus Christ," I interrupt because I've just spotted a porn scene being filmed on the dance floor. "Look at those two. Do they ever give it a rest? It's like fucking dogs in heat."

"Says the dog in heat," she mutters, turning around to check out what I'm referring to.

"At least I keep my debauchery on the down-low. I don't need everyone checking out my moves."

She laughs. "Your moves. Ha."

"Don't mock what you don't understand, Blondie. *Won't* ever understand."

"And you don't mock what *you* don't understand. Like that kind of unbridled, authentic passion," she returns. "If you've never been in love, you don't get…that's assuming you haven't…"

"I haven't." Proud card-carrying member of that tribe.

She turns back and her lip curls a little. "But they are kinda gross."

My mouth curves into a smile. "Two more," I call to the hot barkeep.

Once again, I slide a drink Lisa's way, and once again she pounds it. She kinda looks like I feel. Like I've felt for the past couple of months. Ever since the phone calls started coming in. A little bit weak, a lot distracted. Sick to my guts. I roll my eyes at what I'm about to do. "You wanna hang out or what?"

Her eyes come up and meet mine. "Excuse me?"

"You know, while those two grope the shit out of each other. You and me. Hang out and drink."

Her chin lifts and she studies me. "I thought you wanted some tail."

I don't tell her I already got some. Maybe cuz I don't want to think about why the fuck I walked away from some easy head. I shrug. "I'll take a night off. Give my dick a rest."

"Oh, Vincent. Your charm and manners dazzle me."

"So, is that a yes, Blondie?"

She sighs. "Well, I don't seem to have a better offer. But can we switch to tequila? If I'm not going to remember tonight, I'd at least like to wake up among the living tomorrow."

I order us T-shots and when they come we clink glasses and toss 'em back like sailors on leave. Or two people who have heavy shit on their minds and need to go comatose. I signal for another round—actually what I signal is to just keep ‘em coming—and when they do and I hand Lisa a glass, our fingers touch. They’re soft and warm, and I sorta pretend like the feel of her skin doesn’t do anything for me. When in fact, it gives me a slight chub.

“Thanks,” she says.

“Sure.” I put the glass to my lips, then stop. “Hey—and Blondie?”

Her eyes lift to meet mine. They’re wide and the color of ocean water.

Here I go. My soft side coming out as the alcohol goes right on in. “You’re hot as fuck. Like the mind-whacking kind. The kind where a dude isn’t satisfied even if he jacks all night long because he wants you again.” There. That should keep the shoulders up, the tits out and the tears at bay. I jerk my chin at her. "Cheers."

My eyes won't open.

I mean, really they won't open. I think they're fused shut. And my tongue…it's doubled in size. And there's a taste. My stomach rolls.

Oh, god…it's coming…

I turn over in my strange, blind state, grab whatever's beside me and barf into it. The pressure makes my eyes slam open, and the sight and smell of my vomit makes me retch again.

"Ohhh…" I moan. Head. Pounding. Need…I dunno. What do I need? It's been a long time since I wasted myself. Addy will have a cure. In the blender. She always has a cure.

I swallow and wipe my mouth off with the sleeve of my…no sleeve. No sleeve? Wait…that was my skin. Oh, shit. My dress is still on. I slept in my dress.

"Fuck me," a male voice beside me rasps. "That smell…not cool, Blondie."

My heart stutters. Male voice. I know it. How do I—Blondie.

BLONDIE?!?!

Oh, no…

"Vincent?" I eke out as I glance over my shoulder.

"Don't yell," he grinds out.

He's lying beside me, fully dressed, shadow of a beard, eyes at half-mast as he stares up at the ceiling.

My stomach rolls again. “Oh, no. No, no, no, no.” Trash can, wherefore art thou?

“Voice. Blondie. Down. Please. Fuck.”

The smell of the trash can wafts toward me and I shove it away. I can’t throw up again. I need fresh air. A shower. Advil. For my head…and my lips. Lips? I reach up and feel them. Swollen and sore. Why?

My heart descends rapidly into my stomach. “We didn’t…?”

“What?” he utters. “Drink the entire bar? Maybe.”

“Not that. Did we…you and me…” I can’t say it.

“God, no.” He sits up and winces. “And after seeing that performance of ‘Drunk Chick: the Morning After’ we never will.”

Something moves through me. Not sure if it's relief or feeling affronted. "Where are we?" I demand in this strange, high voice that doesn't at all sound like it belongs to me. I think it belongs to my old friend, Tequila. She used to be so kind…so forgiving… "Is this your apart—" I stop because, seriously, where are we? I glance around the room. Except it's not exactly a room. Leather club chairs…tiny windows—

Someone clears their throat behind us and I jump, then instantly feel like ralphing again.

"The plane landed twenty minutes ago," she says. "We didn't want to wake you, Mr. Vincent."

Mr. Vincent? What the hell is happening? Am I still sleeping? Plane? I sort of work myself into a sitting position and face the woman who, by her clothing choices alone, I'm going to guess is a flight attendant.

My guts clench. What in the hell have I done?

"What time is it?" Vincent asks her.

"Ten a.m., sir."

Sir? I try to piece this strange puzzle together. Did Vincent hire someone to fly us somewhere last night? And why? What were we both thinking? Oh, god…my gut rolls. Again.

Vincent's on his feet now. How has he done it without falling over or ralphing? And why does he look so fresh? Well, not exactly fresh, but decently put back together. I can't even imagine what state I must be in.

"What time did we board?" he asks, running his hand through his fauxhawk.

The woman looks a little sheepish. "Around four a.m. Las Vegas time."

I shake my head and plan my course of action. Standing is up first.

"I know I didn't instruct anyone to go to the airport," he says. "So how did we get here?"

"Town car at the club. It was waiting outside, and you asked the driver to take you home. With your…" Her eyes move over me. "Guest."

Okay, seriously, I'm going to puke again. So many things wrong with this. First, was I actually going to Vincent's place with him last night? Clearly he hadn't planned the airport thing. And second, I'm pretty sure this woman thinks I'm a hooker.

"So, she's been having me trailed," Vincent says.

I look up. I'm on my hands and knees now. Almost there… "Who?" I ask him.

He ignores me.

"I suppose we can't refuel and return to Vegas?" Vincent continues. He sounds different. Older, maybe? Cleaner?

"I'm sorry, sir," the flight attendant says. "I do have instructions to return you tomorrow, however."

"That doesn't help, Carrie."

Carrie? He knows her? What is all this? Am I in some alternate universe? He didn't hire her? He did hire her? My brain is fuzzy—along with my tongue.

"I apologize, sir."

"It's not your fault. I know who to blame for this whole thing."

"Vincent," I try to yell, but it comes out sounding like an animal's cry of pain. Which is sorta right on the money. I've had enough. I'm confused and tired and weirdly hungry yet vomity too, and I want to know what's happening. I want to know how we got here, why we were brought here and where Addison is. My eyes catch on something under one of the club chairs. Is that my purse?

When I look up again, Vincent is staring at me. He looks dark and miserable.

"Where are we?" I say.

His jaw tightens. "Minnesota."

What the fuck? My stomach plummets and rocks. "Why? How?"

As the stewardess disappears, he releases a heavy breath. "There's a party here I've been asked to attend. Forced, is more like it."

Still confused. Really, really confused. "Whose party? I don't understand any of this—"

The plane's door opens then and sunlight suddenly blasts inside the cabin.

"My mother and her husband," he says.

Mother? He has a family? I mean, of course he does, I guess. I just always think of Vincent as descended from wolves. Or vultures.

"They've been blissfully and ignorantly married for fifteen years."

"So…what? This is an anniversary party?" I push myself to stand and walk over to him. "And why do I think you'd rather be anywhere else?"

His nostrils flare. "Because I would. Come on."

We stumble out of the plane and hiss at the light like two vampires who just exited their coffins. Squinty, I descend the stairs behind him. Cool morning air greets me and I breathe it in. Fresh air. Country air. Minnesota air? I see that a town car is waiting on the tarmac like we're flippin' royalty or something, and for one second I wonder just who the hell Vincent is. Because, I mean, look at all of this. Private plane. Sleek black town car. Does the tatted and pierced boy with the sexy eyes and filthy mouth have secrets?

Methinks so.

As the driver waits by the back door of the car, someone emerges from it. She looks somewhere around forty-five and is pretty conservatively dressed.

"Is that your mom?" I ask.

Vincent exhales heavily. "My nanny."

My mouth falls open as I hit the bottom step. And as I watch, the woman comes right up to him and pulls him into her arms.

VINCENT

Just the smell of this state makes my skin crawl, and yet I need to keep the windows open. Blondie and I don't smell so hot. And speaking of Blondie…

I venture a glance in her direction. She's staring out the window. Her red dress is dirty, her hair is wild—and admittedly kinda sexy—and she's missing a shoe. After she realized it, she ran back up the stairs and into the plane to look for it. Never found it, though. She does however have her purse. Which is more than I got. My phone is in my pocket, but my wallet is gone—which is bad. Going to have to cancel everything when I get to the house.

The house.

Their house.

We exit the highway and head for the 'burbs. I haven't been back in years, but everything looks the same. The Lunds grocery store where I always used to get those sour cream muffins after smoking a blunt with my friends. And farther up, miles and miles of white fencing and some of the most beautiful horseflesh in the country.

My head is aching fierce now. Can't believe I'm giving in, giving up after all these months of pushing her back. Granted, she went rogue getting me here—but I'm not calling Rush and making him book me a ticket, now am I? I'm letting this car take me to the one place on earth that rattles my bones.

Kelly is staring at me. Probably wondering what the hell happened to me. I was all preppy haircut and virgin skin when I left.

"It's so good to see you," she says to me. Like she means it. And my guts get tight.

"You too," I say.

Her gaze flickers in Lisa's direction. "Is this your girlfriend?"

"No," Lisa answers instantly.

I sniff, grin. "Don't hurt yourself with that swift reply there, Blondie."

She turns and acknowledges me, then Kelly. "I just want to be very clear."

"It was just a one-night thing," I say.

Lisa's mouth drops open. "No it wasn't." She turns to Kelly. "No thing. Or…night." She groans *oh my god* under her breath and brushes a hand over her face. “We were out with friends. We got…separated.”

“What we got was shitfaced,” I say.

Lisa groans again.

Kelly laughs. “It’s all right. I understand. I was young once.”

My eyes connect with hers. My nanny. A real mother to me when mine was adrift on new and mind-altering love. “What are you still doing here? Working for them?”

Something steals that gentle light from her eyes. “Private secretary. To them both. And with your mother’s—”

“Right,” I say quickly.

Lisa jerks her head in my direction, gives me a look. She doesn’t like that I interrupted Kelly. Thinks I’m a rude asshole. But what’s new? She doesn't need to know everything. Details and shit that are none of her business.

The car turns onto the drive and I glance up. Pinpricks of something I refuse to name attack my skin. Like someone trying to squeeze all the ink out of it. Sunlit green lawn and ancient trees, a spotless tennis court and a picturesque pond, surrounded on both sides by Gable Lake, give way to my family's twenty-two acre estate. Nothing's more beautiful than this place.

Nothing's uglier than it either.

As soon as we stop, Kelly gets out of the car and heads inside. She knows I need a second. Fuck that. I need another five years.

"You going with her?" Lisa asks me.

I don't answer. Just gesture to the driver to close the door.

"Okay." She turns to face me. "Spill. What the fuck? What is this place? Looks like a resort, and that's saying something as I come from the land of mansions." Her eyes narrow. "Are you rich? Does your family live here?" She shakes her head like she's trying to make sense of it. Good luck. "Did you grow up here?"

"Fuuuuck." I drop back against the seat. I don't wanna. Just…don't wanna.

For a couple of seconds, she just sits there. Waiting. Staring. Then she exhales loudly, grabs her purse and opens the door. "I'm going to call a cab and head for the airport. I gotta get back. Check in with Addy. I'm sure she's freaked out."

I stay plastered to the leather seat like a pussy. "All right."

"All right?" she repeats.

Jesus H. Christ. "Yes, all right." I let my head fall in her direction. "What am I supposed to say?" *That I feel like a fucking infant? All I need's a car seat and a binkie with a skull on it? That my heart is slamming against my chest so hard right now I might drop unconscious? And that admitting any of those would be a helluva lot better than having to go inside?*

"You're supposed to tell me something," she returns hotly. "We're sitting in a town car in front of your family's…estate? In Airno, Minnesota—"

"Orono," I correct.

"Whatever," she grinds out. "I woke up like an hour ago on the floor of your family's private plane. I'm pretty sure they kidnapped us? Like…back at the bar…" She groans and scrubs a hand over her face. "I'm confused, and nauseous, and probably look like a broken-down hooker. And I don't belong here. I'm sure you agree. So, good luck to you, and maybe I'll see you back in Vegas."

She starts to get out of the car, but I stop her. "Wait."

Shit, I stop her. I must be dire.

She turns back, glares at me with her raccoon eyes. "What?"

That's right, douchebag. What are you going to say? What do you want? I mean, she's set to go, so let her go. You don't need her. This will all go to shit whether she's here or not, so... "You look like a good hooker."

Her head draws back. "What?"

I shrug. "Like the friendly, straight-up high-class escort type. The kind Tiger Woods would have on speed-dial—"

"Going now."

"Wait." I reach out and grab her hand. Fucking me. Vincent. V. The Asshole. Needs No One. Nada. *Jesus.*

She stares down at my hand. Wrapped around her hand. Soft, warm skin brushes my palm.

"You should stay," I say.

Her eyes flip up to meet mine. In this light, this bright, chipper Minnesota light, they're summer-sky blue. And her hair, though sticking out all over the place, shines like the motherfucking sun. She's a mess. Kicked out of bed and walking home at eight a.m. kinda mess—though I can't imagine anybody kicking her out of bed. Blondie screams cuddle time. Then fuck-me-again time. Then shower-with-me time.

I continue, though my boxers are feeling a little tight. "Like, at least until after breakfast. And a shower." I shrug again, try to play it off as nothing more than basic consideration. "Every legit sex worker deserves a shower."

That last comment earns me a glare, but there's not a ton of heat or hate behind it. She's tempted, yet she's weirded out by this whole thing. Which I totally get. I'm weirded out too. No idea what's waiting for me on the other side of that hand-carved-in-Peru front door.

"So?" I push. "You'll stay? For a hot minute?" I flash her an attempt at a charming smile.

Her eyes are working me over now, probing me. And not in the good way. "You want me there as a diversion, don't you?"

"What?"

"You don't want to go in there. You're fighting it hard. Clearly, you have issues with your family or—and probably more likely—they have issues with you. So you want to use me." She sort of half laughs. "As if my barf breath, raccoon eyes and hair issues are going to distract from the tats and the piercings, and the hair and the clothes."

I frown. "Fine. You're right."

"Course I'm right."

"Get outta here, then. Off with you, slut."

She smirks. "I do need a shower."

I slide my gaze her way.

"And a shoe," she continues.

I nod. "Yeah, that would be hard to explain to the TSA."

"I just don't get it, you know? Where did it go?"

"What?"

"My shoe! I looked in every crevice in that plane. I wish I could remember. This is all so humiliating."

"You have no idea, Blondie." I grab the handle on the car door—the trigger—and pull. "No idea at all."

Oh, hypocrisy, thy name is Vincent.

As I step into the foyer of the main house, in my rags and one shoe, and take in its classic-lined vastness and gold-plated splendor, I remember all the quips and digs the guy standing beside me once lobbed my way. Back in Santa Barbara nearly a year ago for my graduation. He was wearing a shirt with something super inappropriate on the front, jeans that made his ass look mouthwatering—*Hey! Don't veer off course here, Lis*—and all he wanted to talk about was getting Kevin some ink. On his white-bread skin. He didn't actually say that last part, but it was implied. I mean, he was all about making fun of the blue blood.

And lookie here. He's one himself!

Mr. Vincent. I say it in my head with an English accent and an exaggerated bow.

Before I can get too carried away, a woman appears. Not like she beamed herself into the middle of the room or anything, but she came in so quietly I'm not sure where she emerged from. Anyway, she's dressed in a perfectly pressed gray uniform. My mother would approve.

"Would you like to wait in the library?" she asks us.

"No," Vincent says.

I elbow him and whisper, "Rude." Then I smile broadly at the woman. "Thank you. We're fine here."

"Where's my mother?" Vincent asks.

“She’ll be down in a few minutes.” She looks at me. “Can I get you something while you wait.”

A shower? Clothes for the sunlit hours?

“We’re fine,” Vincent says, though it’s practically a growl. And when the woman leaves—ah, I see, down a hallway to the left—I cut him a look.

“Can you chill out a little?”

“What?” His eyes bark at mine. They’re really black, and pissed. And, if I’m not mistaken, nervous.

“I’m here,” calls a voice from the top of the stairs.

Vincent stiffens, and I feel his hand brush against mine. I look up at him. He’s staring at the staircase, his strong jaw tight. “You okay?” I whisper.

"Fucking brilliant."

For some strange reason I take his hand and squeeze. But he jerks it away.

Fine. Just trying to help.

"I'm so sorry to keep you both waiting." The woman who is descending the staircase is probably around fifty or so, but she looks older. She's tall, thin—very thin, the kind of thin my mother covets—and perfectly put together. Dark blond hair cut short and stylish, clothes off the runways in New York. And shoes…I sigh…shoes to drool for.

When she hits the bottom step, her eyes cut to Vincent and she smiles. But it's not a loving, my-little-boy-is-home smile. It's wary and cool.

"Charles." She looks him over. "It's good to see you."

First of all, I don't think it is. And second, *Charles*? I look up at him. His skin is pale under all that ink. I stifle the urge to grab his hand again. I need to chill out too. I'm sure whatever is happening here is just the same thing I deal with from my parents. Disappointment in how one's offspring turned out.

"You look well," she continues. "Though it is a little hard to see you under all that…paint."

"Ink," he says.

"Excuse me?"

"This is ink, not paint. It's *in* my skin, not *on* it."

She nods, her gaze resuming its inspection. Granted, she hasn't even acknowledged my presence. Not that I blame her. My mom would probably toss a sheet over me right now and pretend I'm winter furniture.

"Are you taller?" she asks.

"No."

"I think you are." She smiles, and this one actually seems to reach her eyes. "You've grown at least two more inches. Wait until your father sees you."

"My father's dead."

I gasp. I couldn't help it. Jeez. Talk about cold. I swear in all the times I've heard Vincent—or is it Charles?—get pissy or go off on people, I've never heard actual venom come out of his mouth. It startled me. And from the look of it, his mother too.

Her nostrils flare. "Your stepfather, I mean."

Vincent says nothing.

Finally, she turns to face me. She has that blank, false, serene expression I've seen a thousand times on all my parents' friends' faces when they could care less about who you are but manners and propriety dictate that they have to ask. She extends her hand. "Emily Birch."

I accept it and shake it gently. Despite her tough-as-nails attitude, she seems frail. "Lisa Whalen. It's nice to meet you."

"Yes," she says as if she agrees. "I was only expecting my son, but it's lovely that you both came to celebrate with us."

"We didn't come here," Vincent says in a bitter tone. "We were brought here, like prisoners of war."

Emily laughs. "Oh, Charles." She says to me, "My son doesn't visit very often. He's busy."

Vincent sniffs. “Right.”

“So I must insist,” she continues. “You raise them to leave the nest, but when they do, it’s difficult.”

“Sure,” Vincent says. “Must’ve been difficult for Kelly.”

Mrs. Birch pales.

“Toldja you wouldn’t want me back here, Mother.”

Oh dear… This whole thing is crazy uncomfortable. And combined with the headache, hunger, and a desperate desire for a toothbrush, I’m looking for exits. Where did that maid beam off to again? I wish I understood what the deal was with Vincent and his family. Knowing him as I do, this could easily be some bullshit thing where he didn’t get what he wanted back in the day, flew off the handle and ran.

But my gut tells me it's something deeper.

Something darker.

"Well," Mrs. Birch says in a strained singsong voice. "I'm sure you'd like to freshen up. I have rooms made up for the both of you. They have private baths, of course."

"You can't be serious," Vincent says.

"Or, I suppose, you can stay together, in the same room if that's—"

"No," I start. But Vincent cuts me off.

"We're not staying here at all."

"That's absurd."

A maid who is coming down the stairs stops, assesses the situation and quickly turns around and heads back the way she came. *Take me with you!*

"Where are you going to stay?" she continues. "We're sixty miles from town."

"Sounds perfect."

Her chin lifts. "Charles."

It's like a tennis match. And the name. His real name. Seriously? Nope. I can't get used to it.

Clearly, neither can he. "It's Vincent," he hisses.

She ignores him. "If you don't want to stay in the house, that's fine. You and your…friend—"

Ouch. Just say it, Mrs. B. *HOOKER*.

"Lisa," he says with another shot of venom. "She told you her name. Don't pretend you don't remember it."

"It's fine," I say, taking a step back. I'd really like to go. Shower and eat elsewhere. "Really."

"It's not fine," Vincent says. "She's being a condescending snob."

"Charles," the woman warns.

"I know what's going through her mind." He turns to me and grins. It's a black, pain-laced grin. "If she only knew, right?"

I seriously can't believe I'm here right now. In Vincent's family house. It's crazy. I should be in Vegas with Addy—or better yet, Napa with Addy. You say yes to hanging out, drinking a little, and look where that gets you.

Mrs. Birch has decided to continue as though Vincent hasn't said a thing. "You and *Lisa* can stay in one of the guest houses. Take the one farthest away if it'll make you feel more at ease. I'll have clothes"—her eyes dip to my feet—"and shoes brought over."

I shrug. Nicely played.

"Not necessary," Vincent says, pulling out his cell.

"I think it is. The young lady—"

"For fuck's sake, Mother, it's Lisa!"

Mrs. Birch gasps. "Language, Charles."

It isn't until just that second that I realize Vincent hasn't said one crude thing since his mom came down. He's been plenty rude—no doubt—but he hasn't cursed. Clearly, he's got some modicum of respect left in him for her.

He punches something into his iPhone, then stuffs it back in his pocket. "What time is the party?"

"Eight o'clock," she tells him. She looks flushed and upset. I hate this whole thing.

"We'll be back at eight." He turns to go. "And we'll be gone by eight fifteen."

I'm sorry, what? We? Party? Tonight? I look from him to her and back again. Damn him—damn them. Damn my love of tequila. I'm not supposed to be here. 'Hanging' with Vincent. Or Charles. Or Sir. I'm supposed to be in Napa getting a salt scrub.

Even though Vincent is already out the door, I nod at Mrs. Birch. "It's nice to meet you."

She grants me a tepid smile. "And you. Lisa."

For one brief second I toss around the idea of telling her I'm not a hooker, that I'm really the prodigal daughter of a prominent Santa Barbara family, but whatever. Why do I give a shit what she thinks of me? I hurry after Vincent. Out into the cool Minnesota air. I'm expecting the door to the town car to be open and waiting, but there's no car.

And Vincent? He's halfway down the circular driveway.

Oh, for fuck's sake.

I hobble after him. Cursing with each sharp pebble I encounter.

"Stop!" I call.

And to my surprise, he does. Though he looks like he really doesn't want to. Well, too damn bad. We need to hatch a plan here. And find a ride. And shoes…

I'm about to call him Charlie as I reach him, about to tease him regarding the gold-plated life he's clearly kept from everyone, and maybe joke about rich parents and their stuck-up, demanding ways—because I've got plenty of experience when it comes to that. Anything to sort of lighten the mood and get us talking about what we do from here on out.

But I don't do any of that. Because Vincent is...well, he's shaking. As he stares out at the driveway, Vincent, the hardest of all hardasses, is actually shaking.

What the hell? I glance back at the house. The boy's got fear and anxiety, and maybe some anger going on? Not totally sure, but oh, yeah, this is about more than just a teenage Vincent being an asshole and leaving the home of two older assholes.

I turn back, scrub my hand over my mouth as I decide what to do. What to say. This is the guy who pulled his hand away from mine when I tried to comfort him. Who says crude, thoughtless shit at the drop of a hat. But then again, this is the guy who stripped away his usual thick and slick armor to ask me to go into his house with him. So…shit.

I come to stand beside him, but don't touch him. I stare out at what he's staring at, and say, "Let's get out of here. Okay?"

"Fuck." That's it. That's all he says. But I kinda know what it means, so I whip out my phone. Hit the Uber app.

"What's the address here?" I ask.

"16 Forestberry Lane."

I get to typing, making the arrangements. We'll hit the city, scoop up a decent hotel room and figure things out.

"That's going to cost some serious green, Blondie," he says. "And I don't have my wallet."

For some reason this makes me smile. "No wallet. No shoe. Smelling like the inside of a dumpster. We're quite a pair." I drop the phone back in my purse. "Hot messes, baby."

He turns to me, trains those dark, intense eyes on mine. "I'm serious. Don't have anything to give." He looks tired, but still unbearably sexy. How does he manage that? Maybe it's the being just a little bit vulnerable.

"I know," I say. "I got this." I lift a brow. "Okay?"

He stares at me for a second. The shaking's not as obvious—maybe because it's just below the surface of his skin now. I can't even imagine what's going on behind those obsidian eyes. In his brain. His heart. I want to ask. I want to know what drove him out of that house besides the cold mother. But I don't.

"Okay," he says finally.

And after a minute or two, we walk to the end of the driveway and wait for the pick-up.

VINCENT

I follow Lisa into the suite at Minneapolis's Garrison & Fifth Hotel. She's picked the largest, most expensive digs in the place, with two bedrooms, two baths, a movie room and a wet bar. But I barely notice. Barely care. I'm fucking tired. Wrecked, as the kids say. And instead of giving her shit for setting us up in style, I head straight for the corner of the room where it's darkest and plant my ass on the floor.

It's a crazy move, like a mopey toddler or something. But sitting on anything else, going anywhere else, feels like I'm connecting to the world or something. And I'm so not connected. I'm seriously unplugged.

I'm hoping Lisa walks right on past me to one of the bedrooms, closes the door and gives me an hour or two to screw my head back on. But she doesn't. In fact, she's still over by the entryway. Watching me, yet pretending she's not. I fucking hate that she's here. No. That's not exactly right. I hate that she had to see that bullshit with my mother. I don't give a fuck that she knows my blood's as blue as hers—probably more so—because I'm not that world anymore. I walked away from it and didn't look back. Until the world started calling and texting, and guilting the shit out of me.

"You hungry?"

I'm tucked into the corner of the suite's living area, the floor-to-ceiling windows to my right. I want to shut down. I want her to stop looking at me, talking to me. And I really want her to quit the pitying me. That's probably the worst part of this whole deal. The one chick who's always disgusted by me, maybe a little bit afraid of me—and maybe a lot turned on by me—feels sorry for me.

It takes everything I got to look up, look at her, give her a grade-A douchenozzle grin and let fly, "I could eat, baby." I let my gaze drop to her tits and I force an ogle. "Get that dirty dress off and that fine pussy over here and feed me."

For a moment, she's taken aback and I sense victory. Or at least peace. *That's right, Blondie. Same ol' V.* So walk right on by, take your shower, buy some shoes.

Go home.

But again, she doesn't. Just exhales.

"You hear me?" I say, an edge to my voice now. "It's play or get lost."

"No," she says.

My gut twists up again. "No what?"

"No, we're not doing that today." She drops her purse on the marble table in the foyer, kicks off her remaining shoe and heads my way.

Motherfucker, she's a pain in the ass. I should call Rush. Make him…oh, shit—what? Fly out here with my crap? Buy me a plane ticket back? Hold my hand?

Lisa's hanging out at the minibar now. So maybe she's gonna grab herself a drink and head for the room or the shower. Nothing like a cocktail while you wash. But of course she's not. That would mean she's cool and chill and not desperate to be all up in my business. As I watch, she takes everything—and I mean every fucking thing—out of that stocked minibar and fills her arms with it.

Then she brings it over to me and dumps the entire lot—candy, little bottles of booze, chips—into my lap.

"Fuck me," I utter, hands up, stunned.

Undaunted, she sits down on the floor across from me. "You promised me breakfast. And since neither of us got any at that fabulous and surprising lake shack of yours, this'll have to do." She snags a package of Oreos from my lap and a bottle of vodka.

"We could just order room service," I say.

"Very true…Charles."

I wince. Fucking hate hearing it cross her lips. I'd tell her so if it didn't involve explaining the why of it.

"Come on," she pushes, opening her cookies. "At least give me that."

I exhale and look away. “It’s my real name, okay? Real first name. Whole thing is Charles Henry Vincent. Vincent was my dad’s name. After he died, I chose to use it.”

She pauses with a cookie halfway to her mouth. “Sorry.”

I shrug. “It’s fine.”

She doesn’t believe me. I can see it in her eyes. Probing. Probing. She’s like a guided missile, sensing my hot/weak spots. I cut her off at the pass. “Didn’t you want a shower? Like yesterday?”

She’s also smart as fuck too, so she knows what I’m doing. “I’ll get there.”

“We could take one together?” I suggest, licking my lips. “Or I can get you wet right here.”

“Oh, Jesus,” she breathes. “Just stop, okay? It’s pointless.”

"Coming on to you is pointless?" I laugh. Real bitter. "This I know." I drop back against the wall.

She eats another cookie. "You're not coming on to me, Vincent. You don't want to talk to me about what the fuck is going on here, so you're trying to get me to run. You're deflecting, to quote the therapist my mother forced me to see when I was twelve. I have a feeling you've been deflecting a lot in the past several years."

I ignore that last part and ask, "Why'd she want you to see a therapist?" I can't help myself.

She shakes her head. "I'd just gotten my period and she wanted someone else to explain all the changes I would be going through."

"Nice."

"Yeah, they were super nurturing and stuff."

I snort and grab one of the munchkin bottles of vodka. “Our parents would pretty much have wet dreams over each other.”

She laughs, then eyeballs me. “Come on. What happened, Vincent? Why did you leave? Why don’t you visit? I mean she’s a total cold fish, but I’m guessing that’s not the reason.”

“Just not the life I wanted to live, that’s all.”

“Nah,” she says. “That’s very fortune cookie-y and self-aware, but it’s not the truth.”

I down the entire bottle. “You’re not going to analyze me, Lis.”

“Already done,” she says, grabbing another pack of cookies. “You’re hurting, like, hardcore. And instead of dealing with it, talking about it, letting it out, you ask me to sit on your face.”

I lean forward until our noses are about six inches apart. "I never said that exactly. But it's an idea…and a righteous visual."

"Ass."

I grin. "Don't forget the 'hole.' I never do."

She shakes her head, her eyes connecting with mine. They're some good-looking peepers. Deep blue and heavy on the emotion. I could maybe drown if I ever went swimming, you know? They flicker down to my mouth then, and I feel a kick behind my zipper. The cock is curious. Has been since I first met this chick. But she'd said no, and I don't work for pussy.

She has some dirt on her ear, just a little, but it calls to me, and I do something unbelievably stupid. I reach out and run my thumb over it, the lobe and a little of the shell. Jesus, it's her fucking ear, not her clit, but my cock doesn't seem to understand the difference and it goes all granite.

Cursing under my breath, I drop back against the wall again and utter in a disgusted voice, "Can you go do something? Eat your crap elsewhere."

She eases back too, her face a little flushed. "There he is. The poster boy for deflecting."

"I wasn't deflecting, Blondie. I wiped some schmutz off your ear, and it got gross."

"Schmutz?"

"Time for that shower, is what I'm saying. You need it."

"Oh, god, I so totally do," she agrees.

But does she go anywhere? Fuck. No. My cock is the only one who's pleased.

"So, did you guys not agree about your future?" she continues, snatching up a bag of hot cheese curls. That's gonna hurt later. "Was it the tattoo artist career choice? Totally disappointed them? And just so you know, if there's anything I understand, it's disappointing parents."

I sniff my disbelief and my annoyance. "Sounds to me like you're a model daughter, Blondie. Staying in town, marrying a Dipshit McFancyPants, settling down, living next door."

"It's not next door. It's six houses down."

"Shit, I was kidding. Seriously, you're going to live on the same street as your parental units?"

It's her turn to frown. "Why not? Who cares? I'm doing what I want to do. I made a choice—"

"Oh, get off. You can't bullshit a bullshitter, Blondie." I grab another bottle from her lap and drink the whole thing down in one swallow. Hey, if she's going to insist on staying here and bothering me, I'm going to get drunk again. "What's the rich asshole's name? Maybe I know him. Turns out I know a lot of rich assholes." I grab another bottle and give her a cheers. "Turns out I am one."

"You know his name. I told you yesterday at Wicked Ink. It's Kevin, and you've met him."

"Doubtful. When?"

"At my graduation."

My head comes up so fast I almost give myself whiplash. "No. Fucking. Way." I start laughing. "Not Buttons."

"Stop."

"Oh, Lis, you didn't. The guy with the perfect puss and the pastel and the parents?"

She looks uncomfortable now. *Well, welcome to my world, honey.*

"He's a good man," she says.

I snort. "He's still wet behind the ears."

"He's older than you."

"Wet. Behind. The. Ears. Has nothing to do with age." I take a swallow of whatever this is in my hand. "Speaking of wet—"

"Let's not."

"How's your pussy when he's touching you? Slip and slide, or Sahara?"

She points a bottle at me. "I'm not discussing Kevin with you."

"What about your pussy? Can we discuss that?"

"No."

I exhale, drop my head back and look her over. "Where does he think you are right now? Does he know you're in Minnesota? Does he know you're in a hotel room with me? The asshole with no morals who wanted to ink his milky white ass the last time we were together?"

"No."

"You should tell him."

"Why's that?"

"Because maybe he has a right to know."

She laughs. "Oh, okay, Mr. No Morals." She shakes her head at me. "Why do you care about any of this, Charles?"

"What do you mean?" I ask, though I pretty much know exactly what she means and I'm…deflecting.

"Why do you care about Kevin?" Her brows go up in challenge. "His skills? His knowledge? His white ass?"

"I really don't."

"Then stop talking about it."

"Hey, pretty tits, I didn't want to talk about my family and you kept right on pushing."

"That's different."

"How?"

She pauses. "I don't know. Because…we're here. Stuck here. Dealing with it. With them."

"You don't have to be." I want to bite the words back the second they leave my mouth. She could so easily say, *You're right. I'm out. Face the fire on your own, dickweed.* And if she has any sense, she will.

But thank fuck she has no sense.

"We have things to do, Mr. Vincent," she says, climbing to her feet. "Shoes to buy. Real food to eat. Friends to connect with and let know we're alive and together and staying the night."

I can't hide my surprise. "You're really gonna go with me tonight?"

"Yes, I'm going," she says with a touch of irritation. "So get out of the corner and reengage. I'm going to go take a shower. Finally."

"Good idea," I say, my lips twitching. "I've smelled dumpsters with a better odor than you."

"Once again, your charm overwhelms me."

And with a quick flip-me-off, she leaves the room. Leaves my eyeline. What she should be doing is leaving this suite—and this state. Why isn't she? It's not like I'm all that cool with her. Frankly, I'm a douche. I should've insisted she go back to Vegas. She really doesn't belong here, in this mess. And yet, I can't help myself. I'm relieved as fuck.

I push the bottles and snacks off my lap and slowly get to my feet.

Lisa

Addy: Minnesota?!? Like on purpose?

Me: Not exactly.

Addy: wtf does that mean? R U okay? Mayb u should call me!

Me: I'm fine. V and I got a lot hammered and ended up here. His fam is here! Long story. Later.

Addy: No now! I thought you were dead!! Or abducted! Or…

Me: W/ Vincent?

Addy: :(I was praying it wasn't that.

Me: Well, stop praying, beeyotch.

Addy: When r u coming home?

Me: Vegas isn't home.

Addy: U know what I mean. And tell V Rush is super pissed. He missed—

"'K. I'm here. What are we doin'?"

My head jerks up and I slam my phone against my chest. I'm in the middle of the sidewalk, a couple buildings down from the hotel, and Vincent is standing right beside me. How did I not hear him?

I slip the phone into my purse. Vincent watches it go. “White Bread?”

“Addison.”

“Rush pissed at me?”

“Yeah. How’d you know?”

“Five messages on my phone I haven’t listened to.” He scrubs a hand over his jaw. His unshaven jaw. “I missed an appointment this morning. Or maybe Janie handled it all by her lonesome.”

“You could just tell him the truth about what’s happening,” I suggest as a kid on a skateboard whizzes by. It’s actually kinda awesome here, in Minneapolis. Funky and cool, hip and interesting. Who knew?

"Pass. I don't need Merrick all up in my business." He gives me a pointed look. "And keep BC out of it too."

I roll my eyes. "You're such a pain."

"Backatcha, Blondie."

"Let's just get to work. Take my credit card and find something suitable to wear." I point at his clothes from last night. "Because you aren't going to walk into the party with that on."

He makes his one pierced eyebrow go up and down. "Would serve 'em right, wouldn't it?"

"Well, it wouldn't serve me right. You smell. The shower barely helped." I glance down. "For the both of us. I had to borrow these shoes from the concierge. They're a size too small which is making me cranky." I thrust the Visa at him. "Now take it or suffer my wrath."

He pretends to pout. Looks good on him. But really, what doesn't? "I feel like a prostitute."

I shove it into his hand with an impatient breath. "Welcome to my world."

He stuffs his hands in the pockets of his jeans and sorta gets flirty with me. "So, I can get what I want? Whatever I want?"

I play along. "That's right. Go make yourself pretty for me, sugar cock."

His eyes widen, and then he breaks out into some serious laughter. Like, the belly kind. "Oh my god. Shit, Blondie. Your mouth. Damn."

I toss my hands in the air. "What? Doesn't work on me?"

His laughter downgrades to a smile. "Actually, I think it works just fine."

Did I say that the smile is killer? Crazy sexy? Like if we were into each other and he was holding me and smiling at me like that, I'd strip. And possibly beg.

My heart flips over just once inside my chest. Kind of like it did this morning when he touched my face—well, when he wiped schmutz off my ear.

"Hey," he says, trying to grab my attention.

"Yeah?"

"I didn't say thanks yet. So…thanks."

The grin is gone. And the way he's looking at me now sorta freaks me out. It's not his usual brand of staring. Like, hardcore ogling of my lady parts. This is like…friendly. Like…we're actually friends. Could such a thing be possible?

I blow it off as nothing with a wave of my hand. "You're welcome."

"I'll pay you back, you know?"

"Oh, I know."

He looks up at me through his lashes. They're dark and long and frame his black eyes like liner. He's so sexy and intimidating and hot…and needs new clothes and another shower.

"And for…you know," he continues. "Going with me tonight. You didn't have to. Don't have to."

I raise my brows and act like I've just won the lottery. "Oh. Okay, then. Making other plans right now." I tap my temple. "In my mind. Making the plans."

He grins again—seriously good look on him—and puts one palm on the brick beside him. His inked biceps are distracting. "And what plans would those be?"

I inhale deeply and sigh with thoughts. "An in-room massage, followed by room service, a bubble bath and then…Pay-Per-View."

He snorts. "That all sounds boring as fuck."

"Well then it's a good thing you won't be the one enjoying them."

"Lis," he says, kinda leaning toward me. "Thank you."

He's too close. And despite the need-another-shower thing, he's like triple-layer chocolate cake to a chick on her third day of a juice cleanse. Oh so tempting. And then there's the being all nice and charming—the real kind of charming. I must put an end to this. "Okay, off with you, man candy," I say, pointing down the street. "Find your Mustache Rides shirt and Balls on Display baseball cap, and get your hair colored hot pink and your nails done in blue and green stripes. And I'll see you back at the hotel."

He pushes away from the wall and grins. "I'm gone. But honey, if a bath and massage is what you're aching for—"

I shake my head. "Didn't say ache. Never said ache."

"I'll take care of you, is all I'm saying. I'll help you relax."

My body instantly erupts. And I mean, *erupts* into flame. It's like a match on lighter fluid in there. "Something tells me your kind of massage ends up with the opposite of relaxing."

The grin widens and he says in this low, husky voice, "If you're lucky."

And… *Kaboom! Smokey the Bear, where the hell are you?* Again, I point to the street. "Go."

"Fine." He starts walking. "Stay out of trouble," he calls back. "At least until trouble gets back to the room."

I watch him. I watch him walk all the way down the street and into one of those shops for skateboarders. Me and a few others. He's a sight to see. And drool over. And the thing stirring around in my stomach—the thing that was in there last year when he showed up at my graduation—it breaks open and moans with lust and want and wishing and don't-you-dares.

Shaking my head at myself and the inner workings of my stupid, reckless, bonfire of a body, I turn around and head for Saks.

VINCENT

The suite is like a tomb when I get back. Except for the A/C coming on, going off. No doubt Blondie is still hitting the stores. It's a well-known fact that people with vaginas can shop for hours. No break needed. I fucking hate it. The worst part? Hauling a bunch of bags home.

I throw said bags on the couch and head for my room. Before the girl gets back and tries to dress me or some shit, I want to get a few ZZZs. But the second I open the door, I'm greeted by a shriek. Guess the girl's home after all. My vagina theory is way off, man.

"Wrong bedroom! Wrong bedroom! Oh my god! Get out, Vincent! Jesus!"

I close the door. Well. Hmm. That was a motherfucking eyeful. Nude Blondie. Not something I get to see every day. But definitely something I wouldn't mind seeing every day. I inhale real deep. My dick is growing inches *fast*. Jesus H. Christ that woman is luscious. Like, I would lick that like a popsicle on a hot day.

My mind is just rewinding and replaying as the door opens and a towel-wrapped Lisa emerges from her room. She looks pissed and pink. Good combo. Just sayin'. And I got it now. Yup. *Her* room. Just, you know, next time put a sign on the door.

"What did you see?" she demands, lifting her chin. She's totally makeup free and her hair's piled up on her head.

"Nothing." My lips twitch.

"You're lying—*and* you're laughing."

"Am not." I'm trying to control my mouth. Seriously, I am. Just like I'm trying to control my thoughts. But damn…those legs, and that ass. And shit, don't get me started on the tits. My fucking hands are making grabby twitches.

She's got Glocks in her eyes as she stares at me. "You're laughing at seeing me naked."

"What? You're cracked."

"My body parts are heinous to you."

Fucking pink body parts. Shaved body parts.

Vincent wants.

"Is this what you didn't want to tell me at the club?" she continues with her nutso ranting. "When I asked why I'm not getting male attention anymore? I've gone downhill in my old age?"

"You're twenty-one."

"Two," she corrects. "Twenty-two."

I contemplate grabbing the towel and yanking it off her. Dragging her into the bathroom and showing her some male attention. Right in front of the mirror. Ba-Boom! "Why are you so fucking insecure all of a sudden? Last year you practically shit overconfidence."

"Gross."

"It was kind of annoying."

"It was annoying because I turned down your offer of a threesome." She pauses. "Or was it a foursome?"

I shrug.

Her mouth falls open. "You can't even remember?"

I wag my finger at her. "You're deflecting, puddin'."

"I am not."

"We were talking your lack of confidence, remember?"

"Not funny," she says.

I lean against the wall. "No. You're right. Actually, this is pretty serious." I squint like I'm thinking real hard. "You're confident in your hotness, then you're not. What happened? Or who?"

She sees right where I'm headed and cuts me off at the pass. "Don't blame this on Buttons."

"His name is Kevin," I return with fake-ass disgust.

She gasps. Kinda looks mortified. At herself, methinks. Then with an indignant sniff, she pulls her gaze from mine and stalks past me, heading for the living room. "You're just fucking with my head."

I follow. Christ, I want to put ink on that back. "At least I'm getting in somewhere."

"Ha! You're never—" She stops near the couch that's holding up all my bags. She stares at them a sec, then whirls around. Her eyes are all over me—my clothes, my face. "You got your hair cut."

I run a hand over the clip and style job I ordered. Miss the 'hawk already. "Just a trim."

Her lips parted, she comes up to me, stopping when she's an inch away. She smells fucking fantastic. Something fruity. Juicy. I can feel the heat off her body and my dick is begging for a sniff of her too.

She reaches up and puts her hand on my cheek. "And a shave?"

I flinch. "What are you doin'?"

Her eyes just keep on roaming. "And you took out your earrings and…your eyebrow rings." She runs her thumb over my brow, then her eyes lift to mine. "Why?"

I'm not all that good with people touching me these days. I step back. "Maybe I wanna be Kevin for the night."

She sorta does this laugh/sniff thing. "No."

"He'd have a much better time. Would fit right in too, amirite?"

She's staring at me. Maybe a little confused about my clean-up. Maybe a lot confused about why I backed up when she touched me. "I don't want you to be Kevin, Vincent."

Good to know. "No?"

She shakes her head.

"You like me just the way I am, Blondie?"

Her lips twitch cuz she knows I'm hitting the humor now. "Well, I wouldn't go that far."

"Come on," I push. "Admit it."

She cocks her head and really looks at me. "Okay." Then she adjusts her towel. Again.

My grin and playful shit I was laying on her recedes. I'm waiting for it, you know? The bite back. The punchline. Any second now, yo. Blondie's got a million of them when it comes to me. *I like you just the way you are, Vincent. A total asshole whore who lives in another state.* Ouch. Oh yeah. Hurts so good.

But she doesn't go there. Not even a little. All she says is, "You know, it's getting late. I'm going to finish getting ready."

My brows drop and I stare after her. Sorta flinch again when her door closes. Okay. Maybe I need to rethink some shit here. No ink on that smooth, soft back. No cleaning schmutz off her ear. And the hard dick? Right Hand will take care of it in the shower.

My eyes lift again to that closed door.

I'm being a thoughtful dick. Flirting and coveting that hot ass. But what if Blondie does like me? Like, really. That'd be the worst. Some chicks are just cool with fucking and walking away. Those are my kind of chicks. And not only is Lisa not that chick anymore—maybe she never was. I mean, she did turn down my perfectly awesome proposal last year. She's getting married in four days.

I may be an asshole. But I'm not a total slime. And this girl is cool. Helped me out today when I was drowning. Leading her or pushing her or whatever I was doing just now is fucked up. I'm gonna nip this in the bud, and make sure Mrs. Buttons gets to the church on time.

No detours. Onto my face. Or into my bed.

No matter how much I'm fucking aching for it.

The dress I picked is a stunner. I knew it would be. Elegant and sexy, perfectly fitted, it's strapless, mid-thigh and ice blue to match my eyes. And the shoes…dear baby Jesus, the shoes. Silver, crystal-beaded Manolos. *Dies*. Dad's going to flip when he gets the bill, and wonder what I was doing in Minnesota, but that won't be until after the wedding. So whatevs. Party now, pay later.

The old Lisa is back, bitches!

With one last look in the mirror to check my makeup, which is subtle and slightly smoky, and my hair, which is pulled off my face in a sexy low bun style, I leave the bathroom. I'm a little nervous to see Vincent. Or have him see me. I can't believe I care about impressing him. He's such an ass, and will probably make some comment about this dress not giving me enough titty cleavage. I laugh as I head into the living room. Can't help it. That sick bastard's got me crushing something fierce.

But he's not there. My heart flips over. *He's probably ironing his Clit Tease University Graduate shirt, so find something to occupy yourself, and your raging hormones, while he does.* I grab my purse and go over to the table in the foyer, start transferring the contents of the old into the new one I bought today. It's small and sleek and just basically holds the essentials. Lipstick, mints, powder, condoms—*kidding!* I'm nearly done when I hear a low whistling sound.

I glance up.

And flip the fuck out.

Only on the inside, of course. I'm not a total tween. On the outside, I'm rocking the cool-as-ice vibe.

Well, melting ice is more like it, actually...

But seriously, the guy is—

"Wow," I say on an exhale of absolute appreciation. He grins and walks toward me. When I say this is a Vincent I've never seen before, I mean it. One hundred percent. This is...businessman Vincent. Fifth Avenue Vincent. It's tailored black suit on long, lean, ride-you-all-night body. And silver tie and crisp white shirt against ink. It's just a hint of ink—on his neck and hands. It's fucking perfection, and I just want to attack the shit out of him.

"That's what I say," he tells me. "Wow." His eyes run over me.

Totes wolf eyes. I'm drowning.

"You look smokin', Lis."

Make that exploding. From pleasure. It's exactly the reaction I was praying for. "Thank you."

He kinda moves around me. Wolf stalking prey. "You're so…perfect. I want to mess you up." His eyes lift. "Can I mess you up?"

Yes! "No, you may not."

He laughs. White teeth, black eyes. Good god, he's hot. Private confession moment: I've never wanted to kneel down in front of a guy and just…I don't know, go to town. Unzip and do things I've only read about or watched on that spankavision channel my first college boyfriend had in his dorm room. But with Vincent, I do. My mouth is watering.

"You're staring at me like I have two heads," he remarks, straightening his tie.

No, not two. I was just thinking of the one. A shiver goes through me. Shouldn't be thinking of it, but there it is. "So. Where's the mustache shirt we talked about?"

His lips twitch. I stare at them. "They were out."

"Bummer."

He nods. "I won't stop my search, though."

"I'd be disappointed if you did. I'll keep on the lookout myself."

He comes up behind me then. I can smell him. He smells so good. "Find it for me, Blondie, and you get the first ride."

I try to stifle the gasp, but it comes out sounding like a cough. "Giddy up."

He laughs. “Should we call Uber or what? Get this freak show on the road.”

“Actually,” I grab my purse and turn around to face him. My freak. For tonight, anyway. “I got us a car.”

His metal-free brows lift. “Well, don’t I feel like fucking CinderINKella.”

I laugh as I grab the key to the room and hand it to him. “Now, if only you had a glass loafer to lose at midnight.”

“Oh, Blondie, we’ll be out of that house way sooner than midnight.” He opens the door. “Now off we go.”

VINCENT

After my dad died and my mom married her financial advisor, Garrett Birch, we started having these dinner parties at the house. I think for my mom it was her way of getting back into life, or solidifying her new relationship, or some shit like that. But for me it was a big fat bummer. I usually stayed in my room and cranked the tunes or played video games until it was all over. Lotta pizza in those days. Anyway, the parties got so fucking popular that people were coming to the house nearly every weekend. It was a complete bitch and a half. Until my mom started making me go. Then it was ten fucking bitches. Talking to strangers, rich assholes who were pretty much plastered and desperate to tell a fourteen-year-old kid all about the hot piece of ass they had waiting for them after they ditched their wives. *Yeah, fucktard, you're a super stud. Keep downing that Viagra*. If I could manage it, I escaped to the pool house. Hung out. Read. Drank. Hell, I was fourteen. Until one night when the Step-Fuck came looking for me.

Not to drag me back to the party like you'd think.

And not to help out my mom either.

"Working in a tattoo parlor," the woman standing in front of me is saying. "That must be very interesting."

"Pays the bills," I answer distractedly. Where is Blondie? She was with me a second ago, and then Kelly came over and wanted to show her my baby book. My fucking baby book. Do they still have that? My mom didn't burn it or some shit? Kelly must've saved it from the flames.

Before talking with my former nanny, Lisa had given me one huge smile, rubbed her hands together and said, "So many blackmail possibilities."

I laughed. Cuz for that one second I forgot where I was. No. That ain't right. I forgot what had gone down here. I glance around. The woman who had been chatting me up about my job is gone now. *Sorry, ma'am. I'm not fit for company.* The house looks…well, fuck, like it always looks. Perfect. Dripping bling. Ice sculptures and cater waiters, shining chandies overhead, and four bars five-guests deep. Let's celebrate, ya'll.

I spot Lisa and my chest chills out a little. Not sure how she does it, but she makes the air inside this house breathable for me. I stare as she walks toward me. I mean, who wouldn't, right? That dress is criminal. She looks like a fucking angel. No. Strike that. Reverse it. She looks like an angel I want to fuck. Bad V. Very bad V. Not two hours ago, I was telling myself I wasn't going to screw with that. I really am an asshole. But fuuuck me, I'm taken with her, you know? I mean, how do you just turn that off?

Halfway to me, she gets waylaid by three old chicks who are all over her shoes. Granted, they are fucking badass. Three inches of do-me-now. And if I was going to forget all the shit I said about not pursuing the future Mrs. Buttons, I'd oblige those shoes. And make sure she kept them on while I spread her out on my bed and ate her right—

"Charles Vincent." The voice is female and unfamiliar, and I want to call her a fucking pain in the ass for interrupting my fantasy moment regarding all things Lisa. "You came home," she continues.

I finally look her way. She's about my age, skinny, petite, dark blond hair and huge tits. Yawn. Her eyes move over me. "And looking like that. Well, aren't you brave."

I'm gonna try real hard not to be a dick. "Do I know you?"

She pretends to pout. "Minnie O'Neil."

I shake my head. "Sorry."

She moves in closer, brushes those tits against my chest and whispers, "The art room. Last day of senior year at Tally Day Prep."

Oh yeah. Mutual handjob on Mr. Davis's chair. "Right. Minnie. With the mouse." Aka her clit.

She beams. *Jesus*. "You remember?"

"You made me call it that." Come on, how long does a discussion about shoes last? I need my Blondie over here. It's been way longer than fifteen minutes and I'm pretty sure I'm turning into a pumpkin.

I make the mistake of looking up then. Near the stairs. And everything on me goes rigid. It's the couple of the evening. They're moving through the crowd like royalty. The respectable Birches. My mom looks put-together, but pale. And her eyes are kinda dull even when she smiles at her friends. I feel a twinge of something in my chest. She's sick. Maybe a year, if she's lucky. It's the reason for all the calls and the texts. Why she really wanted my tatted ass back home. Knew she wasn't getting me here for anything else except maybe her funeral. After all that's gone down between us, I really want to not give a shit. Kinda like she didn't give a shit. But I'm here, ain't I?

My eyes shift left. I'm hoping for nothing but dead air as I stare at him. But I'm not that lucky. Or that skilled. My skin is getting tight around my bones—like it's fucking anticipating being touched. And I have this frantic urge to run.

They're coming at me now. Hand in hand. The couple of the night. A solid marriage that nothing—and I mean *nothing*—can tear apart.

"Well, Charles," my mother says when they reach me.

"Mother."

"Look how tall he is, Garrett. Didn't I tell you?"

"You told me, Bunny." That voice. It's the fucking one of nightmares. Freddy Kruger and

Jason and that chick from "The Ring" all rolled into one.

"And so handsome," my mother continues. "Now if only he hadn't done that to his skin."

Garrett's watery green eyes catch me and hold. My gut dive bombs into my groin. "You do look like something on the side of one of those abandoned buildings over in Briar Creek, son."

My head is pounding. *Son.* Jesus Fucking Christ I might puke…

"Charles?" My mother sounds annoyed. Probably because I'm not talking. But I can't breathe. For fucking real.

I look over and see Lisa. Still surrounded by those three women, she's staring at me. Instantly, she notices whatever the hell is plastered on my face. Shock. Fear. Panic. She mouths, *What's wrong*? But I got nothing for her.

Panic is filling me up like ocean water and I rip my gaze away. *Fuck. Not you.* I don't want her anywhere near this. I shouldn't have brought her.

My heart is slamming hard and fast inside my chest. All I hear is a buzzing sound. I shake my head to get rid of it.

"Charles, you're being very rude," my mother is saying. But I'm barely listening. I have to get the fuck out of here.

I'm going down.

Shit.

I make a split-second decision. And it's a bad one. I know it. But that doesn't stop me. I'm the king of bad decisions. I grab the hand of the chick I was talking to when Mom and Step-Ass came up—

Minnie and her Mouse—and I lead her out of the room.

THE GIRL WHO'S WANTED TO FUCK CHARLES VINCENT SINCE HIGH SCHOOL

We're in the library. It's dark except for the light of the full moon coming in through the windows behind me. I'm breathless with anticipation, and the top of my dress is pulled down around my waist. He did that to me. The second we got in here.

But that's all he did. *Bizarre.*

Now he's across the room, leaning against a shelf of books and looking at me like I'm an alien. He, on the other hand, looks like dessert. Normally I wouldn't pursue someone with tattoos. It just screams bottom of the pickle tub, if you know what I mean. I'm not keen on contracting one of those diseases people who use needles have. But I know where Charles comes from.

And what he'll inherit.

"What's wrong, Charlie?" I coo. Is he playing hard to get? Is he a voyeur? Should I start?

He doesn't say anything. Just stares at me. No. Through me.

I moan and grab my breasts, start massaging them. I've got small tits, but they're perfect. I've been told that more than once. In fact, everything on me is perfect. I've been told that too.

"Oh, yes," I say with little, breathy moans. "This feels so good." I give each nipple a pinch and gasp. Men love this. Watching women get themselves off. Or at least start the process.

Well, most men.

What *is* happening? I pout, and try the little girl routine. "Minnie Mouse wants to come out and play, Charlie. Is that tongue of yours pierced? Because I know she would just love—"

His foul curse cuts me off. He pushes away from the bookcase and stalks over to me. *There we go.* I grin and release my breasts, raise my hands above my head. Baby voice is always a guaranteed winner. *Men.*

But he doesn't go for it. He…what the fuck is he doing? "W-wait," I stutter. "What—" He's pulling my dress up. He doesn't want any of this. He doesn't want me?

Not possible.

"Go," he says, backing off again.

I stare at him, my cheeks burning. “You’ve got to be kidding. You’re a fucking Dorothy from Kansas, aren’t you?”

He turns and faces the bookshelf. Gives me his back.

“Screw this,” I say and head for the door. “You’re an asshole.”

“Yeah,” I hear him utter as I walk out in a disgusted huff.

I want to hate him. Actually I want to leave and pretend these past two days never happened. Starting with Addy's abduction. But I can't. This guy has sorta become my friend, and there's just something about this situation that doesn't compute. That look on his face while he was talking to his mother and her husband—right before he grabbed the girl's hand and dragged her away. I've seen that look before. On him, in fact. During the shaking episode outside the house this morning.

The door where the girl just came out is ajar. Vincent's still inside. I know this because I've been standing here since they went in. Did they do something? Did he fuck her? I don't know. I didn't hear anything, and it's barely been ten minutes, but what does that prove? Clearly he didn't take her in there to show her his first edition King James Bible.

"Shit," I utter as I break with self-preservation, not to mention pride, and walk into the room.

Even in the dim light, I spot him instantly. He's sitting in a leather club chair, his back to the windows. It's just too dark and I head for a floor lamp and click it on. Warm yellow light spills into the room, and his head snaps in my direction.

"Why are you still here?" he says with a sneer.

Asshole. I walk over to him. Not a hair is out of place. "It's only for a couple more minutes, sunshine."

"Good." He pulls me onto his lap, and in seconds his mouth is crushing mine.

At first, I'm too surprised to do anything but assess. Then I realize what's happening and rip away from him. "Jesus, Vincent." I stand up. I'm breathing heavy. "What the fuck are you doing?"

He just stares up at me. So casual. Totally unaffected. "Come on, Blondie."

I point at the door. "You just had another girl in here."

"So?"

"Oh my god…" I must be insane. Seriously. To even have followed him in here. To give a shit. "I'm taking the limo back to the hotel."

He looks away and pushes out an annoyed breath. "Fine."

"And then to the airport," I continue.

"Should've done that this morning."

My mouth drops open. I have so completely misjudged this guy, I'm sickened. "I'm out." I turn to go.

"Jesus Christ," he calls after me. "I didn't do anything, okay?"

My hands go up as I head for the door. "Not my business."

"I wanted her—"

"Just shut up."

"I don't mean I *wanted her* wanted her." He curses. "I wanted *that*. Whatever *that* is. What it used to be. The thing that turned off my mind and soul so I could fucking function."

That last sentence hangs in the air as I hit the door. It makes me stop. He can't function? Dammit. And the tone of his voice. No more asshole, couldn't-give-a-shit Vincent. Whoever this is, his voice is small and young. And hurt. I close my eyes and breathe in. I shouldn't care. I mean, I really, really shouldn't. He just admitted to me that he came in here with that random chick so he could fuck away his feelings.

Am I nuts? Or just trying to get myself good and hurt?

I stand there, frozen in the doorway for a good three minutes. I want to go—and yet I don't want to leave him. Not until I know what's behind the anger and the shaking and the self-medicating.

"Will you talk to me?" I say, though my eyes remain on the door.

Silence.

"Will you tell me what happened? Did she have a temper when you were younger? Did she hit you? Scare you? Tell you how worthless you were?"

Another couple seconds of silence, then, “No.”

He’s not going to do it, is he? Not going to tell me anything? Hell, maybe there’s nothing to tell. I want to go. I need Addy right now. My hand reaches for the knob.

“She pretended her husband wasn’t raping me nearly every weekend for three years.”

My guts drop to the floor and every inch of my skin is goose bumps. I whirl around and slam my back against the door. I know my eyes are wide and huge as I stare at him. And when our gazes meet there is absolutely no question that what he has just said is true. Tears gather in my throat.

“He should be in jail.” My voice is a whisper.

His eyes are stones. “He should be six feet under, but dreams don’t always come true.”

"We have to go to the police." I point behind me to the door. "He's out there. Walking around. Like…like it's nothing."

Vincent is up out of his chair and coming at me. "It's pointless."

I shake my head.

"She'll lie for him." He's in front of me now.

"You don't know that—"

"I'm the liar, Lis," he says, his eyes probing mine. "I made it all up because of my grief over losing my dad. I didn't want another man taking over that role, so I accused him. I punished him. That's what she told me when I told her. Every time I told her. When I begged her for help. When I showed her the bruises. When I showed her…"

My heart is beating so fast I feel sick and lightheaded. It all makes sense now. How cold she is. How angry he is. And Vincent had to come back here. “Why? Why did you come here?”

“She’s sick. Cancer.” He sniffs. “It’s all she wanted. Her perfect little family, together again. For everyone to see.”

Oh my god. I take his hand. “Well, fuck her. We’re going. Right now. We’ll figure out what to do later. You don’t owe her anything.”

He walks with me, down the hallway and into the foyer. It’s totally deserted now. I can hear voices coming from another room to the right, but I couldn’t care less. I need to get him out of here.

But he stops in the center of the foyer and turns toward the noise.

“You don’t need to say goodbye,” I tell him. “You don’t need to say anything.”

His fingers lace with mine and he squeezes my hand. I can barely breathe. There's fresh air outside. Away from here.

"Vincent," I say and try to tug him toward the door.

But he's not listening. He's refusing to go.

"What are you doing?"

"Come on." Still gripping my hand, he takes off toward the sounds of the party.

"Wait," I say. "Don't go in there."

But he doesn't answer. Just keeps going. I try and keep up with him, my heels clicking on the marble floors. There's nothing I want more than to get out of this place. It's like a beautiful, cold prison. And I can't stop envisioning a young boy—with no one to protect him. No one who believes him.

We break into what looks like a massive dining room, but with a hundred people instead of the table and chairs. There's a buffet at one end of the room and at the other end, a raised dais. My stomach drops as I stare at it. Emily and Garrett Birch are up there. Celebrating, surrounded by their friends. Someone slips glasses of champagne into our hands. A microphone is going around.

"...congratulations, Bunny and Garrett. We love you."

"...a couple of such incredible integrity. We are so grateful to have you as friends."

I can barely stand it. What lies. They should know. Everyone should know.

Applause breaks out. And oh god, I think Vincent is thinking the same thing because he drops my hand and when I turn to see why, I notice he's got the microphone now. The blood drains from my face. Everyone is turning to look at us. At him.

"Mom," he starts. "Garrett." He lifts his face to the dais and addresses them. "Congratulations on fifteen years of marriage."

He sounds completely normal. Controlled. But I can feel the heat coming off his skin. And I know beneath it, he's trembling. The Birches are watching him with total ease. They aren't worried at all. I want to wring their smug necks.

"All of your friends are gathered here to celebrate such an achievement. The love you two share. The bond that defies anything and everything. New family unit…cancer…the sexual abuse of your only child." I gasp. And I don't think I'm the only one. "It's pretty incredible." He pauses and raises his glass. "Fuck the two of you very much. May you drown in pain and suffering for the rest of your lives for what you did to me. I know I will."

In the palpable silence, Vincent drains his glass then drops it on the floor. The crash is our exit, and when he leads me out of the room and down the hall toward the front door, I can't hold on to it anymore. I burst into tears.

VINCENT

She's stripping me.

Motherfucking Blondie. Lisa. The chick who rejected my threesome—and I'm pretty sure that's what it was. The girl who got me out of that house tonight. She's taking care of my ass. Her eyes are red from crying, which she did for about fifteen minutes on our way back to the hotel. I held her hand while the waterworks went down because A: she seemed to need it. And B: I seemed to need it.

Tie's off and she tosses it over the chair. Suit jacket, same deal. Then she starts in on the buttons of my shirt. Her hands are coming real close to me and I'm not sure how that's gonna work. I'm damaged inside and out these days. The no-touching thing, it started after I left home, but got worse a few months back when my mom contacted me. It was like a black cloud moved in and refused to leave. Squatter's rights, yo. Just setting up camp, twisting my mind every time I was fucking someone. I didn't want their hands on me. Eyes on me. Didn't want to talk.

Lisa kills that last button and slides my shirt off. For a sec, she just stares at my chest. Got a lot of ink there. Not even sure there's any blank canvas left. The light in the room is on dim, but I'm sure she can see it all. The words, the black and gray scratch marks, the dragon flipping her off. She's so uptown I kinda don't know if this turns her on or not. She reaches for me then, and I wait for the flinch to come. But when her palm makes contact with my abdomen, all I feel is heat. My eyes close for a sec and I just breathe. Cuz, again, with her I can. Motherfucking Blondie. Is she my savior or what?

“Do you ever wonder about these?” she asks me.

My eyes flip open and I stare at the top of her head. “What do you mean?”

“Why you got them? Why so many?”

“I love ‘em. They’re fucking art.”

She nods. “They are. Especially this one.” Her fingers brush over the lower part of my abdomen, through a bit of my happy trail, and my breath kicks. It’s a piece I did myself. Of a hawk sitting on the Virgin Mary’s shoulder. It hurt like a motherfucking bitch on steroids.

“But I can’t help but wonder,” she continues. “If maybe they’re also…armor or something?” Her eyes lift to meet mine then. Gorgeous blue surrounded by long blond lashes.

"I'm not following," I say. Both her hands are on me now. Tracing my ink. It's distracting as fuck.

"Do you think you put some of this on your skin to protect you?"

My chest grows tight as I get what's she's saying now. "You mean, so he'd never touch me again?"

Her eyes fill with tears, and she nods.

Fuck, this chick kills me. I release a breath. "I never thought of that, but I guess it's possible."

Yeah. I would've pretty much done anything to keep Step-Prick away back then. Maybe moving to another state hadn't felt safe enough. I needed a motherfucking *keep out* sign on my skin.

Her hands fall to my belt buckle next. And even through her tears, she flips it open and off, then tosses it with the rest. Determined girl. Like that about her. Finally, she unbuttons and unzips. Her surprise has those tears drying in a hurry.

"You're not wearing underwear." She looks up.

My lips twitch. I want her smiling again. She's irresistibly hot when she smiles. "Underwear is bullshit." I say.

"Oh, Vincent." She rolls her eyes and smiles.

Hot.

I full-out grin back. *So what now*? I don't ask. I know she sees how hard I am.

Without another word, she just strips me bare and takes my hand. "I'm going to put you to bed."

"I'm thinking you mean that in the boring way," I say, letting her lead me.

She pulls back the covers. "After the night we've just had, is there any other way?"

"Fuck yeah. The dirty way that ends up with my face between your legs."

She sorta pauses then, her eyes on the pillows. "I don't want to be another one of your escapes, Vincent."

I stop too. Because my chest just went tight. I don't want that either. So I don't say anything more. Just let her do whatever it is she's doing.

"Come on, get in," she says, patting the mattress. She ignores my hard on as I oblige, then when I'm back to the mattress, she pulls the covers up to my chin. "There. Snug as a bug."

Who wants to fug, I don't say. Because she's staring down at me. Her eyes still carry the ghost of what went down tonight. Maybe her heart does too.

She's taken it on. My pain. The shit of my past. I'm not exactly sure why, but it's beyond cool. Something no one's ever done for me before. Not that I'd have let them. Lis is different.

"Thank you," I say.

She beams. Like freaking lights up with a soft pink glow of happiness. "See. I knew you'd like it. Being taken care of is—"

"No. No." I shake my head. "Not for this. This is great, but…" I shove the covers down to my waist and grab her hand. "Sit for a sec, will you?"

When she does, I thread our fingers together. Like I did back at the house. I think I want to remind her or something. Or maybe I just dig it. "Thank you. For *tonight*," I clarify.

"Oh." She shakes her head. "It's nothing."

"You know it's not, Lis. It's a huge fucking something." My eyes hardcore connect with hers. I'm not a crier. Never have been, even when I had real reason to. But there's shit going on inside me right now as I look at this girl…tears of the heart or something. It's like, sweet pain. "I've never told anyone what I told you. The things you heard…"

"Is that what you're worried about?" She leans in a little, her expression so sincere it kills me. "It's all safe with me, Vincent. To my grave, okay?"

I shake my head. My chest might actually explode here. "Leave it to me to fall for a chick who's taken."

"Come on."

"I'm serious, man."

She laughs. "You didn't fall for me, Vincent. You're keyed up, emotional. It was a crazy night—"

Okay, that's so not it. And I need her to know that. I can't help myself. I have her in my arms and on top of me in like five seconds flat. Oh sweet, delicious weight. Vincent Jr. is thrilled. He kicks up to greet her. *I feel you, buddy.*

Lisa's surprise registers on a gasp, but she doesn't try to move. Good thing too, cuz I don't think I'd let her. I wrap both my arms around her, vise-style and inhale. She smells like flowers and tears. Fuckin' right, I'm falling.

"Vincent," she starts.

But I'm finishing. "Listen, gorgeous. I can't have you telling me what I feel anymore, okay? Especially when it comes to you."

Her lips part. "I'm not. I'm just saying—"

"That I'm not into you—like in a real way, right? That's bullshit, Lis. We both know it." She's still wearing her hot little dress, and I'm fucking ready to get her out of it. *Fingers, work your magic and find that zipper.*

"I don't think I do know it," she says.

I release her a little. Just to get to that zipper. "Well, here it is. I'm into you, woman. Hardcore. Mindfuck. Possible belief in destinies and soul mate kinda shit. Wait"—zipper going down—"maybe not the soul mate thing."

She laughs softly, but her eyes are imploring me. "And you know, the other bit is I'm kind of…taken."

It's my turn to laugh. She's so funny. Lost her way, I think. Like me. But hey, maybe we can help each other. Find a way back together. "Sit up a sec," I say, releasing her.

She does. Looms over me. And for one moment, I just sorta take her in. Hottest chick on the planet. Especially right now. Hair coming out of that bun, cheeks flushed, tits near to popping out of her dress. And speaking of that dress. It's so getting in my way.

"You want me to compromise you, Lis? You want me to be the reason you have to break up with Buttons?"

Her eyes widen. "Vincent—"

"Cuz I'm cool with that, baby."

She laughs. "I know you are."

My hands come around and grab her ass, hard. "I want you." I lift my eyebrows, give her the serious eyes. "Like, in the real way." And I mean it. I hope she sees how much.

I think she does because her eyes soften.

I yank her forward an inch till she's sitting on my shaft. "Like in a way that kind of scares the shit out of me."

There's a beat here where neither one of us says a thing. We just look at each other. I'm waiting and she's thinking. And that's fine. I'm being real. I want this chick. Like, for my very own. And not just tonight.

After a moment or two, her mouth splits into a gentle, almost shy smile. It's flippin' adorable. "I want you too."

"In the real way?" I tease her.

That smile widens and she pushes up on her knees and starts taking off her dress. *Okay. So the real way. Fuck. Yeah.*

"You want help?" I ask her. Shit, I'm fucking Lancelot over here.

She shakes her head nice and slow.

And I put my hands behind my head and just watch.

Dress comes off first. Over the head and onto the floor. Leaving only a tongue-flopping-out-of-my-mouth matching strapless bra and thong. See-through pale pink lace. My dick is crying already. Poor guy.

"You know I'm going to have to fuck those tits at some point, right?" I say.

"You're so crude," she says, laughing in spite of herself as she removes her bra and tosses it aside.

"And you love it. Look at those nipples. Hard and tight. Proof positive, baby." She laughs and shakes her head again. When she starts to take off her thong I stop her. "Wait."

Blue eyes hit me with lusty confusion. "What?"

I answer in the only way I can in that moment. Jacking up, pulling her against me and flipping her onto her back. Now she's skull to the pillow. Laid out like a fucking Vincent buffet.

She gasps.

Shit, so do I. The girl has a body on her, man. A real woman's body. Curves and ass and heavy tits. It's a wonderland, and V's gonna take his time with the exploration.

I start down at her feet, giving each one a slow kiss as I ease them apart. Her ankles are hot and smooth and I'm a licker. I want to know what she tastes like. Everywhere. And as I do, running my tongue over each anklebone, I see her hands fist the sheets at her side. *That's right, baby. Anchor down.*

I kiss and lick my way up her calves until I get to her knees. The backs fascinate me and I spend a good amount of time there, biting her skin and licking in the crease. It's so hot in there, and with every swipe of my tongue, she jacks her hips and moans.

"Don't fret, baby," I tell her even as my cock is leaking pre-come on the sheets. "I'll get to that anxious pussy of yours. Just have to make sure it's nice and juicy first."

She groans as I move upward. "It is. Dammit, Vincent. It is."

I laugh against the skin of her right thigh. So smooth. "I'm not talking just wet, Blondie. That won't do. I want your cream dripping down..." I run a finger up the inside of her thigh. "Right here." Then I send another finger up the other side. "Here too." The lace on her panties is soaked. I can tell because the pale pink isn't so pale anymore. Maybe I was wrong.

Lis doesn't disappoint.

I grin and keep going, inching my way until my face is hovering over her hot puss. The scent of her distracts me from my slow and easy. I might need to toss that plan and just get to eating. She squeezes her ass then, trying to get closer, and just to make her even more insane—and fuck, me too—I kiss her through the lace.

"Oh, god," she rasps.

"It's Vincent, baby. But people do confuse us at times."

Her head lifts and she glares at me. "This is cruel."

I grin. "Well, I don't want to be cruel." I drop my head and send my nose through her pussy. Even through the lace, she feels me and cries out, head dropping back onto the pillow again. “I could make you come like this. You want that?” Before she answers, I swipe down, and her body spasms. Oh, the things I’m going to do to this girl.

My girl.

Her pussy juice on my nose has pretty much opened the floodgates inside me. I’m unreasonable Vincent now. I want what I want. And that’s her on my tongue. Now. “Don’t move,” I whisper. Then I cover her with my mouth and suck. Her and the lace, into my mouth.

“Oh, god!” she cries.

I don’t try and correct her. Waste of time.

And resources.

I suck her in again. Release. Then again. Four times, until I feel her clit pulse.

Her knuckles are white as she fists the cotton, and she's not heeding my command about not moving. She's squeezing her ass and sending her pelvis forward. Bitch. I grin as I suck on that hot clit. She's going to come. I can tell. And I want to watch. I want to see how she takes climax.

I keep the pace steady as I suck her off through the lace, trying to quell my own orgasm. But those sounds she's making. It ain't easy.

Suddenly, she goes still. Her face, all pink, open mouth—and then she breaks, cries out like a hungry cat and starts thrusting against my mouth. Over and over. It's beautiful as fuck. And wet. Like, really wet.

I'm. In. Heaven.

I don't wait for her to come down. Not my style. I hook my fingers in the thin waistband of her panties and take ‘em down. They join the dress on the floor just as I push Lisa’s knees up to her tits. I want the real deal now. No fabric in my way.

“What?” she utters. “But you already…”

I chuckle and settle myself between her legs. “That was just a warm-up—get the tension O out of the way.” I give her the once-over. She’s shaved and drenched, and I open her with my thumbs and give her clit a little tap. She gasps. “Pink and swollen. Just the way I like it. Now let’s see if you’re ready on the inside too.” I send my tongue up inside of her and groan when her muscles clamp around me. *Oh shit, yes*.

She groans too and I feel her hands on my head. *That’s right, Lis. Hold on. Ride’s about to get wild.*

I replace my tongue up inside her with two fingers, pumping her real slow and easy. And then cover her pussy with my mouth. At first, I try to keep things light because I know she just went off and her clit's sensitive. But it's so hard. I'm hungry and her walls are creaming around my fingers. And my cock is painfully erect. Like blue balls time. It wants inside her before it loses its shit.

Not yet, asshole.

I snuggle into her pussy lips and go to town, flicker my tongue over her clit super-light until she's breathing heavy and trying to fuck my face. Her smell is my personal drug and I can't get enough. But I back off just a bit so I can keep her humming and not falling over the edge again.

"Vincent," she utters on a pretty distressed-sounding moan.

"Yeah, baby," I say before flattening my tongue on her and tugging back and forth.

Her fingers dig into my scalp. "Shit. Yes."

She's creaming hard around my digits. I don't want her coming. Not like this. I want it around my dick.

I ease my fingers out of her, and growl when she cries with the loss of me. *Condom. Condom. Where are the condoms*? I'd put them in the side table drawer, on top of the Bible cuz I'm sick like that. I grab one and rip the fucker open. I can't get it on fast enough. And I'm skilled, yo. Then I settle myself back between her legs, my cock to her wet pussy this time. Instantly, she wraps her legs around my waist and I think I howl with delight. Her eyes are pinned to mine and she's sorta gasping for air.

"I can't believe we're doing this," I whisper, grinning.

She grins back. "And it's only the two of us."

My lips curve into a wicked smile. "Hey, I can find someone if that's what you want."

She tightens her thigh grip on my hips. "Only if it's another dude."

"Fuck that," I say, kinda Neanderthal. Didn't know I had it in me.

"Then fuck that," she returns. She lifts her hips and circles her pussy, teasing the shit out of my dick. "And just fuck me."

This girl. Goddammit. I send my hips back until the tip of my cock is right where it belongs. Then I push myself inside her, all the way. As deep as I can go. Shit, if I could get my balls inside, I would. Then I look down. Her eyes are open. Her cheeks are pink.

Just like her pussy.

I don't move. Not just yet. I'm watching her. Watching her lips twitch, then break into a fantastic smile.

"What? Blondie," I growl, "what do you have up your sleeve?"

She doesn't answer me. Not with words anyway. She tilts her chin up and motherfucking licks my face. I die. And I think I come a little too. Cuz seriously, there's nothing hotter than this girl licking herself off my face. And my lips. And my jaw. I drop my head and go in for the kill. Kissing her as I slowly fuck her. I'm not a huge kisser. Usually I like to get right to it. It's kinda intimate or something. Your breath and their breath intermingling. Looking at each other. Faces you make. I dunno. Always been uncomfortable for me. But with this chick, it's flipped. I want to see everything. Her reactions. I want to know what she likes. What makes her breath catch and her eyes glaze over.

Does that make me a pussy?

Shit.

Or does it make me different than I was a week ago?

A wrecked, tatted-up asshole who didn't think it was possible to climb out of his dark hole in hell, much less change into a different kind of dude.

She wraps her arms around my neck then and I stop thinking about past shit and start moving inside her. She's perfect. A tight fist around my hungry cock. Meeting me with every stroke. All the while, my eyes are open and so are hers. It's so weird. And awesome. Me looking at her while we fuck. It makes my chest hurt. Makes my cock harder. Makes me wish we'd done this a long time ago.

I reach between our bodies then, and as I change the rhythm, grinding myself against her, then thrusting hard and deep, my fingers find her clit and I start up again with some gentle circles. Her breath catches and her eyes flutter. She's going to come again, and I'm gonna be right there with her.

Is this what Merrick has been going on about? Him and Addison? If it is—no, if it's even half of this—I get it. I so get it.

I feel her pussy walls start to pulse around me. "Fuck, Lis," I grind out as I quicken the strokes on her clit. "You keep doing that and I'm done."

"I can't help it," she whimpers.

And then she's coming. And it's different this time. Where the other one was a crash against the shore, this baby is a tsunami. Building, drawing back, then *fuck*…a hot wash of come bathes my dick and I'm gone. I think I tell her to hold on, but I don't know. I'm thrusting hard and quick. Again and again. Deep inside her as my mind shuts down and I'm nothing but a bliss-filled battering ram. Her cries are my own, and I never want this to end.

Even when it does.

Even when her moans lessen and her thighs relax.

I drop my head on her right breast and nuzzle. I want these. I never got to these. My tongue darts out and I lick her tight, high nipple. Then grin when I feel her pussy walls clamp me again. Fuck…

Afraid I'm too much dead weight on her, I roll to the side and take her with me. Instantly, she snuggles up against me, and though I'm not inside her anymore, she still sorta thrusts her wet pussy on my hip. Love it. Shit, who knew? Then she tucks her head into my neck and holds on.

I don't do this. Ever. Stay. Cuddle. Let the sweat have time to dry. And yet I don't want anything else for the rest of my life. I'm a fucking wreck.

As she kisses my neck and mewls softly, my arms go around her. Tight. I'm not letting her go for nothing. Just try and get a crowbar in here, fuckers. This girl is mine. Maybe I'll tattoo that on her ass. Maybe I'll tattoo that on *my* ass.

I grin.

I just have to convince her I'm a changed asshole. That I'm worth walking away from easy, breezy, boring Buttons for.

The grins falters.

I don't say anything about it though. As we cool down and I draw the covers up over us, and she settles in for sleep, I'm mute. Because tonight—of all nights—I can't handle her telling me no. That she's not in.

That she's not mine.

Lisa

This man is so gorge.

I can't stop staring at him.

It's morning, nine something, and I moved the covers off him about five minutes ago so I could really study the hotness. Like, every inch. Every line. Every tat. Honestly, Vincent is *the* most beautiful man I've ever seen. He's long and lean, but muscular too. Like his calves are thick and have a nice amount of hair on them. They have ink too. The left one is completely covered, but interestingly the right one is pretty bare. Just a word scrawled across it. Pussy. *Shocker*. I keep perusing. Up. *Yes.* His thighs are cut—his hip bones too. His stomach and chest are ripped and not an inch isn't blanketed with ink. There are symbols I don't recognize and dragon-like creatures crawling up one pectoral. He likes color. He looks *goood* in color. I keep going. His arms are one of my favorite parts of him. Both have sleeves of tats. But it's more than that. They're strong and corded with muscle, and when they lift me up or hold me close I feel feminine and protected.

And then there are his hands: long and sexy, inked and very, very talented.

My breasts tingle and my sex clenches. Oh yeah, they remember.

My gaze drops to the very fine muscle between his legs. It's hard, drawn up against his abs, and I want to lick it. I glance up. He's totally asleep, his lips kind of swollen from all the work they did last night. I smile and I run my hand up the base of his shaft. Hot, smooth. I wrap my hand around it.

And very heavy.

He groans in his sleep.

That's right, baby, wake up.

I run my thumb over the slit at the top and when a bead of pre-come appears I drop my head and lap it up with my tongue.

Vincent's abs clench. The sight is ridiculously hot and I can't help myself. I guide his cock all the way into my mouth. Deep. *Yum.* Hot, pulsing goodness. My hunger gets the better of me and I start sucking, drawing him in and out of my mouth. Licking him. Nipping the tip until it gives me what I want. A salty taste. I only know Vincent's awake when his fingers slide into my hair and fist.

"Shit, Lis," he hisses. "Yeah. Christ."

His voice is dark and raspy and goes straight to my sex. I give myself up to him, let him set the pace. How fast he wants it. How deep. He's not crazy with that, doesn't send himself to the back of my throat, and I'm grateful. *Show him how grateful.* I lick and suck and moan like I'm tasting the sweetest popsicle ever.

And I kinda am.

And when I feel his body jerk and his cock swell, I don't beg off. I'm not one of those girls. Not with Vincent, anyway. I want to taste him. Just like he tasted me.

"Fuck, you sure?" he asks, his voice pained. He's going to come.

I don't answer, just suck him deep and let him figure it out for himself.

Which he does.

Pretty damn quick.

He comes in a rush of thrusts and groans and curses and hair tugs. So very Vincent. And I love it. Love that I'm making him feel this way.

I don't come off him right away. I savor. Licking the head of him and down the shaft, just to make sure I got everything. But when I do pull back and sit up, he's staring at me, sorta stunned, through heavily lidded eyes. God, he's sexy.

I smile and lick my lips.

He groans.

"Good morning," I say.

"Fuck that. *Great* morning is more like it."

I swear I would stay in this bed with him all day if I could. I want him a hundred different ways. Behind me. Cowgirl, and then reverse cowgirl. And what about my mustache ride? I'm getting that. Whatever it takes.

But there's reality to deal with. I give him a pouty look. "Our flight's at eleven."

He gives it right back. "This, you and me, it's been…"

"Yeah," I finish for him. "Totally."

He comes up on his elbows. "But that other shit…I'm so ready to go back to Vegas." His eyes probe me. "What about you? You ready to go back, Lis?"

I shiver slightly. My body's cooling. Well, that is the question, isn't it? Going back. To Vegas. To Santa Barbara. Here in Minnesota, I have drama and heartbreak and Vincent. In Vegas I have drama too…and decisions…

He sits up and puts his hands on either side of my face, strokes my skin, then slips my hair behind my ears. “I don’t like you quiet, Blondie. I like you loud and snarky.”

My eyes lift to meet his. Black on blue. “I’m not snarky.”

“Please.” He leans in and kisses me. So gentle. So warm. I could get lost. Again.

“The plane,” I say against his mouth.

“Yeah, yeah,” he groans. He pulls away from me. “I’m going. To shower. Alone.”

He stands up and I stare at his ass. Holy fuck. He has those dents in the sides. How did I miss that? And tat free. Me want to bite.

“Did you hear me, Lis?” he asks, glancing over his shoulder. “Showering alone.”

My mouth's watering, so my hearing's pretty much off.

"Stop staring at my ass."

"I can't. It's edible."

He laughs and heads for the bathroom, shaking that fine ass as he goes. I'm going to join him in a sec, see if I can get that from-behind thing under the spray, show him my ass. But first I need to text Addy and thank her and Rush for the first class tickets, and the copy of Vincent's driver's license.

Kudos to Rush for having the thing on file.

But just as I reach for my cell I see a text light up on Vincent's phone. I shouldn't, but I do. Could be one of his—

My guts instantly twist. It's from her.

Mother: You are a true disappointment, Charles. Not the son I raised. That little scene nearly cost Garrett his work. Take your whore back to Las Vegas and never return.

My chest fills with air. And pain. I hate these people. So much it might actually consume me at some point. I pick up the phone. I just can't…not reply.

Mrs. Birch, this is Lisa. (aka the whore) Unfortunately, Vincent can't answer his phone right now. He's at the police station.

Maybe that was wrong. Maybe it's right the fuck on. I don't know, but I leave it there. What happens from here on out is up to Vincent. About those pieces of shit who raised and abused him, and about me. He has choices to make.

I stand up, stretch and head for the bathroom.

And so do I.

VINCENT

Lisa and I are sitting pretty in first class. Unbeknownst to me, she bought us both some chill clothes on her shopping excursion yesterday. So thoughtful. My girl. I turn to stare at her. She looks gorgeous. Kinda bohemian. Tight jeans, white ribbed tank under a cream blousy sorta shirt. Her hair is snaking over one shoulder in a loose braid. And she's got that glow. You know, sex face.

I got it too.

I wonder if her ass is still sore from the shower. Hell, she begged for it. And V's not about to deny L any damn thing. "You miss the private plane?" I ask her.

She sighs. "Please. I don't even remember it."

I snort. "Neither do I."

"Cheers, by the way." She clinks her glass of champs to my beer and I laugh.

"So? You still marrying Buttons, or what?" That's right. I get to it. What's the point of stalling? This one is a need to know before we touch down.

Her eyes are probing mine. Like she's gonna find the answers there.

"Blondie," I start.

"No." My brows go up. Maybe my dick a little too. "I'm not," she continues. "My heart's not in it, and he should marry someone who digs him hardcore, you know?"

Fireworks are going off in my chest, but I play it off cool. "Sure."

"Plus after he hears I slept with you, you know he'll be afraid—"

"He could never measure up?" I interrupt.

She tips her glass toward me. "Absolutely. That."

I chuckle. Fuck, I'm relieved. This girl belongs on my metaphoric lap, like permanently. But she isn't exactly telling me that. Just that Buttons is over. "What are your plans, Lis? Going back to the SB?" The beer's not sitting right in my gut. I put it down.

"Well," she says, looking me over. "First thing, after I talk with Kevin, of course, is to get away from my parents. And then I need to sit down and figure out how I let my life get away from me over the past year. Yesterday was an eye-opener—just the one I needed. And you…I'm proud of you." She reaches out and puts her hand on my right cheek.

"Baby," I turn into her palm and lick it. *Mine. Mine, fucking mine.*

She laughs. "I need to find myself a real job…and you know, get another job while I'm searching for that job."

"We need a receptionist at Wicked. Hella bad." As soon as the words are out of my mouth, I wait for the regret to come. But it doesn't. Shit, I want her there. Merrick is so gonna razz my ass about this.

Lisa is staring at me.

I shrug. "I mean, who else can keep me out of trouble? And…in trouble." I grin.

"A lot of chicks."

"Naw. Not anymore." I inhale. "You done something evil to me, Blondie. The minute you said no a year ago, I was set on making you say yes."

Her drink goes down on the tray table.

"Vincent—"

"Say yes."

Her eyes are just pinned to mine. "If I did—"

"Fuck yeah." Explosions. Like all over the place.

"*If* I did," she repeats. "You need to know, I wouldn't hang on you. I get that you don't want a girlfriend."

Okay, enough of this horseshit. I stand up. "Come with me."

"What?" She looks around at the other passengers. "Where?" Her voice drops to a whisper. "This isn't a private plane, Vincent."

"Ass up, Blondie."

She knows I ain't giving up and takes my hand. I lead her toward the first class bathroom. "If you're gonna be with me," I say for all the flying-in-the-sky people to hear. "You're gonna have to learn to break some rules, baby."

"Be with you?"

I pull her inside the tiny space, shut the door and lock it. I press her back against the thing and get in her pretty little face. "I want you with me. I want you as my girlfriend." It's all I say. I lift my brows. Like, *what do you say to that, Lis?*

But she doesn't say anything. She's mute. And staring. Fuck, I guess I need to make this shit clearer. Always a first time for everything, eh?

"I've made a lot of mistakes." That's a start.

Her lips twitch. "Welcome to the club."

"Okay, yeah, but I've learned some shit too."

"Really?" she asks, lifting her chin. "What's that?" Is that a smile coming?

"Biggest lesson there is, baby." I go in, brush my nose across her nose. "And you taught it to me."

Her eyebrows drift together. "Tell me."

"It's corny as fuck, I can't—"

"Vincent!" She grabs the collar of my shirt and jerks me back to face her. "Don't you dare."

I laugh. "All right, fine." I sober up, my eyes going for the soul now. Cuz I think I got the heart. "Love don't equal pain."

Her lips part. "Love?"

"Okay, okay, let's not put the cart before the horse. You know what I'm saying."

Her smile is wide now. All teeth. "Maybe."

I touch her face. So soft. She's staying. She's got to. "Don't question it, or go all chick in your head about it."

Her arms go around my neck and she bites her lip. She's down with the rule-breaking. Mile High Club, here we come.

"Then what should I do?" she challenges with a smile.

"Just kiss me, Lis," I say as I go in for the kill. "Just fucking kiss me."

Available Now

WICKED INK CHRONICLES

(New Adult Series—17+)

FIRST INK—Book 1

SHATTERED INK—Book 2

Printed in Great Britain
by Amazon

19479801R10150